BREAKING THE RULES

BREAKING THE RULES

GLEN EBISCH

FIVE STAR
A part of Gale, Cengage Learning

MYSTERY

GALE
CENGAGE Learning·

Detroit • New York • San Francisco • New Haven, Conn • Waterville, Maine • London

LIBRARY OF CONGRESS CATALOGING-IN-PUBLICATION DATA

Ebisch, Glen Albert, 1946–.
    Breaking the rules / Glen Ebisch. — 1st ed.
       p. cm.
    ISBN 978-1-4328-2582-9 (hardcover) — ISBN 1-4328-2582-8 (hardcover) 1. Women journalists—Fiction. 2. Historic sites—Fiction. I. Title.
PS3605.B57B74 2012
813'.6—dc23   2011049911

First Edition. First Printing: May 2012.
Published in 2012 in conjunction with Tekno Books and Ed Gorman.

Printed in Mexico
1 2 3 4 5 6 7 16 15 14 13 12

BREAKING THE RULES

CHAPTER 1

Dear Auntie Mabel,

The land next to mine has always been a vacant lot where the neighborhood kids played. Recently, however, I've seen guys in there doing surveys and marking trees as though they're getting ready to build something. I thought this land belonged to the town because it is the only way to get down to the historical monument next to the Ravensford River. I want to make sure that nothing sneaky is happening here. What do you think I should do? Should I confront the landowner with an ax handle and demand that he tell me what the heck is going on?

Concerned Citizen Frank

Dear Concerned Frank,

I would suggest that you contact your local elected officials and ask them to look into this. You might also inform your local newspaper. It may have an investigative journalist who would be willing to check into the matter. I would not recommend confronting the landowner directly with or without an ax handle because that could result in an ugly altercation.

Auntie Mabel

No civic-minded deed goes unpunished. Having responded to Concerned Citizen Frank as I did, Stan Aaronson, our general editor, gave me the assignment of investigating what was going on at the historical site. The first problem that presented itself was finding the spot where history was allegedly made. Interestingly, everyone I talked to claimed to know there was a marker where the first European had stepped on shore and founded Ravensford, but no one seemed clear on exactly where that marker was. I was advised to take the main road out of town, park, and slip-slide down the bank next to the bridge abutment over the Ravensford River, then walk slowly along the west bank of the river. Everyone assured me I would eventually come to something marking the hallowed ground, although, under close questioning, I discovered that no one had ever seen it for themselves.

My name is Laura Magee, aka Auntie Mabel, a name and job I inherited eight months ago when the real Auntie Mabel, the local newspaper's very own advice columnist, died under tragic circumstances, choking to death at the Big Bun on their all-you-can-eat shrimp and lobster night. Having some background as a writer, combined with having recently moved into the area and being jobless, I jumped at the opportunity. It also helped that my grandmother was an old flame of the owner of *The Ravensford Chronicle*. So now at the age of twenty-seven, I get to give advice on life, love, and homicidal intentions to the population of Ravensford, Massachusetts.

At that moment, I was wearing my down vest, a flannel shirt, and the hiking shoes I had bought on the overly enthusiastic notion that I would take long walks in the woods. So far I had only worn them to rake leaves last fall, and not being properly broken-in, they were starting to hurt my feet. I was picking my way along the west bank of the Ravensford River looking for a marker that memorialized the day in 1667 when Jacob Vandersnooten is reported to have established the town. Leaving New York for reasons some have associated with nonpayment of debts, he had crossed what is today Long Island Sound then made his way up the Connecticut River on several rafts that he and those traveling with him constructed. He veered off onto a tributary, looking for the spot where, according to his journal, "A stern but forgiving God would give him succor."

Finally stopping when he reached a point where he could go no farther because of an extremely shallow spot in the river where "one could walk across without dampening the soles of one's shoes," he saw five ravens pecking along the banks. It's said that he climbed off of the lead raft, stood in the shallow spot, and in a "voice like thunder" declared this to be Ravensford. He then walked across the ford and stood symbolically on the bank declaring the land for the Vandersnooten family and God Almighty. Immediately after that, the fleet of four rafts, which held all his family members, hangers-on, and their limited worldly possessions, landed on shore, and everyone fell to his or her knees and prayed.

A historian friend of mine told me that an alternative history is presented in a recently discovered journal kept by the youngest of Jacob's five brothers, Amos. Amos says that his oldest brother did try to walk across the ford, but he slipped and fell, drenching himself in river water, at which time he said a few less than complimentary things about God. He then threw a stone at the pair of crows sitting on the rocks mocking him. When he finally made his way to shore and was about to issue some sort of ringing proclamation, a gathering of Indians on the top of the bank began to throw rocks at the interlopers. Hit solidly several times, Jacob scrambled through chest-deep water back to the raft, and the whole flotilla began to row in reverse.

When they returned and actually came onto the land is lost to history. It also suggests that if the original inhabitants of this land had possessed a few more good pitching arms among them, they might have sent the white man scurrying all the way back to Europe.

This was the level of thought that filled my mind as I made my way along the west bank of the mighty Ravensford. Since the ford had been taken out in colonial times to allow traffic up-river to the Berkshires, there was nothing to go by for the location of the marker except that it couldn't be far from the First Congregational Church. Settlers leaving the Massachusetts Bay Colony for points west had quickly joined Vandersnooten. English by nationality and Congregational by belief, they soon outnumbered the Dutch and built the first church within a relatively short walk of the landing site. I figured a short walk in those times, when everyone walked almost everywhere, could be up to a couple of miles. The First Congregational Church had moved in Revolutionary War times, but there was a stone marking the site of the original, and I tried to mentally orient myself in relation to it so I wouldn't walk endlessly down-river.

I was convinced that I had wandered too far when I came upon a large rock with an odd clump of moss on the side. Picking up a sharp stone, I hacked away at the moss, stirring up the smell of earth and mold. As the green covering gradually peeled off, I saw that there was indeed a plaque underneath that declared this rock to be the one Jacob Vandersnooten leaned upon as he declared this land to be Ravensford. I looked up the slope behind me and figured the top must be the spot where the land was going to be cleared for building. It didn't look like it would be too difficult to climb up the bank and see if anyone was on the property. If someone was around, I might even discover the owner's name and his intentions.

Slowly I began to climb, being careful on the leaf-covered slope. Since I was looking down at my feet, I first thought someone had poked me in the shoulder. I even glanced up in surprise, expecting to find a person standing right in front of me. That allowed me to see the second stone come whizzing down the embankment, hitting me in the shin. Another stone hit me on the other shoulder. Fortunately, the down vest had protected my shoulders, but my shin was giving me serious pain. Staring up the hill and into the shadows, I could barely make out someone standing at the top wearing a blue coat. I saw his arm go back. The next pitch would have hit me in the head if I hadn't seen it coming and pulled my neck in like a turtle. I was starting to develop some sympathy for Vandersnooten.

Deciding it was time to take myself out of range, I turned and ran downhill. Soon my feet got tangled up, and I fell and rolled until I was back at the river. I lay there for a moment getting organized and making sure that no more rocks were sailing past my head. Then I got to my feet. I staggered; my right ankle had been twisted in my downhill slide and was now protesting at carrying any weight. A handy nearby tree limb served as my walking stick as I slowly struggled back along the way I had come. I muttered all the way back to my car, much as Vandersnooten must have done that night around the fire when he realized how close he had been to success, except for a few well-aimed missiles.

But while one might, at least today, make an argument for the behavior of the Native Americans toward Jacob, I felt the treatment accorded me was certainly wrong and probably illegal. I sat in my car rubbing my ankle and thinking up vengeful acts. I wished I knew the identity of the person who had written the letter to me, so we could go together, each carrying ax handles, and settle the score with that landowner.

I have read so many of the original Auntie Mabel's columns that her voice frequently comes to me during times of stress, as it did now.

Wouldn't it be better to put this in the hands of the authorities rather than resorting to violence? If people disobeyed the law whenever it suited them, what would our world be like?

I wasn't sure of the answer to that one, but being, in general, a law-abiding person, I managed to subdue my anger and decided to go to the police.

CHAPTER 2

Dear Auntie Mabel,

My husband Sam runs a one-man computer firm, and he has had the same secretary for five years. They go to overnight conferences together, dine out on her birthday, and celebrate the anniversary of when she joined the company. I am never invited along. I feel rather hurt because Sam never takes me out for my birthday or on our anniversary. I don't like to complain, but should I tell him how I feel?

Left Out

Dear Left Out,

I think you should be more concerned about your husband's constant attentions to his secretary. Its sounds like their relationship is more than a purely business one. You should strongly suggest that your husband not go anywhere with his secretary without taking you along. Unannounced visits to the office might not be a bad idea either.

Auntie Mabel

I walked into the police station, hoping I wouldn't see anyone I knew. If the desk sergeant would listen sympathetically and file the report, I could walk away or, in this case, limp away, having done my duty. Unfortunately, just as I was about to launch into my description of the events to an older, red-faced sergeant, Michael Farantello came walking down the hall and glanced over at exactly the right moment to see me.

"Laura, how are you?" he asked.

I didn't know what to say. When the person who dumped you after a torrid three-month relationship asks how you are, your natural response is to say "fine," because there is no way in hell that you are going to admit that your heart was broken. However, I was there to file a report because something obviously was not fine, and I would sound like a fool to say otherwise.

"Someone has been throwing rocks at me," I said, cutting right to the chase.

Farantello saw the tree branch I was leaning on and his right eyebrow rose.

"Did you get hurt?"

"No, not really. I sprained my ankle a little running away."

His eyes gave me a careful onceover.

"I think I should take you to the hospital to have your ankle looked at. You can file the report later."

I shook my head; no way was I accepting charity from this guy.

"A little ice and some rest. I'll be fine," I asserted.

Farantello reached over and took the form off the sergeant's desk. "Why don't you tell *me* what happened? Let's go into my office."

Figuring that I would appear ungracious to refuse, I limped along behind him, leaning on my rough-hewn walking stick and sporting clothes covered with mud and leaves. I looked like Grizzly Adams on his first visit to the big city. All I needed was a bushy beard.

When I was settled in a chair across from Farantello, I stretched out my leg and winced. He opened his mouth to speak, but the expression on my face must have told him that I wasn't interested in any more good advice. He placed the form in front of him, picked up a pen, and directed an expectant expression at me. Concisely, and with what I hoped was little emotion, I described what had happened to me.

"So there really is a marker down by the river?" he asked when I finished. "I've heard about it but never actually met someone who had seen it."

"It's there," I said, trying not to preen.

"Would you recognize this person who threw stones at you?"

I shook my head. "A blue jacket or coat is all I saw. And probably it was a man, or else a woman who certainly doesn't throw like a girl."

A flicker of a smile passed over Farantello's face. That had always been the way between us: I would try to be funny, and he'd make every effort to keep a straight face. To get a genuine smile or, even more, an outright guffaw, used to make my day. I suddenly felt very sad.

"I'll have a patrol car sent up there to check into this. You're sure?" He pointed down at my ankle.

"I'm going directly home to soak it in ice water."

Farantello nodded.

"How's your daughter doing?" I asked.

He paused, trying to read my expression.

This was a sensitive subject. Our relationship ended when his ten-year-old daughter was diagnosed with diabetes. The girl urged her parents, divorced for over three years, to make an attempt at reconciliation for her sake. I'd met this girl, Andrea, and I have to say my first impression was of a junior-level operator who knew how to push her parents' buttons to get what she wanted. Now that, in addition to all the normal guilt her parents felt about getting divorced, she had the extra ammunition that comes with a *bona fide* illness, Andrea was unstoppable. Farantello and his wife were dating again. He was staying at her house on weekends, no doubt in the conjugal bed. And I was left out in the cold.

Were my feelings hurt? Of course.

Did I feel wrongly treated? Probably.

Was I feeling sorry for myself? Most definitely.

What had led to our final split was when I suggested that Farantello use the wits God had given him and recognize that his daughter was playing them both. His response was a horrified, "How could I say that about a sick little girl?"

I pointed out that being sick didn't make her any less shrewd. And as he was heading in an angry rush for the door, I added, "She doesn't know what's best for herself or for the two of you. As the adults, you should be doing the deciding."

"She's on a special diet right now and will probably have to take insulin," he said, answering my original question.

"Sorry to hear that," I said. "And you and your ex are . . ."

"Dealing with it together," he said firmly, showing me where I stood.

I nodded and struggled to my feet. "Let me know what you find out about my stone-thrower."

"Will do."

I turned and walked out of his office. My ankle didn't hurt so much, maybe because I was hurting more somewhere else.

CHAPTER 3

Dear Auntie Mabel,

My boyfriend told me we should break up. He said that it's not my fault but his because he's just not ready to settle down with one woman. Should I take him at his word or fight to keep him?

Unsure

Dear Unsure,

Some men never know when they're ready to settle down. You have to tell them when they're ready. But before you fight to hang onto him, ask yourself whether you're ready to settle down and if this is the guy you want to do it with.

Auntie Mabel

I was sitting in the kitchen of my grandmother's house soaking my ankle in a bucket of ice water to take down the swelling. When I had first moved here eight months ago, my grandmother and I had shared the house. But she was down in Florida with her boyfriend, Roger St. Clair, the owner of the newspaper where I work. They had left in early January and were supposed to be back by spring. We were in late April now, and there was still no sign of them. I guess old love, just like young love, likes to be alone. I had warned my grandmother that I had taken in as a roommate an old friend of mine from college, just in case she decided to return to the house and not live at Roger's place. Three of us could easily fit, but my friend, Ronnie Blessington, took a little getting used to.

The side door burst open and Ronnie flew into the kitchen.

"I want you to be my sister," Ronnie exclaimed.

I looked up from the magazine I was reading so I didn't have to watch my foot turn into a large white shriveled thing.

"Shouldn't you be at work?" I asked.

"I took off early today," she said breathlessly. "I said I didn't feel well."

I glanced at my watch. "Yeah, I guess eleven o'clock is a good time to call it quits."

Ronnie's blond hair seemed even more tightly curled than usual, and her face was red with either exertion or excitement. Her cornflower blue eyes were open wide and dazed with anticipation, like those of a small child who has spent too much time staring in the candy store window. She plopped down in a chair on the other side of the table as if awaiting my answer about joining her family. The fact that she hadn't asked about my injury did not show a callous indifference to another's pain. She would be very solicitous once she noticed, but it takes Ronnie a long time to take in her surroundings when she's got an idea.

"I'm afraid it's too late for me to be your sister," I explained. "Your parents and my parents are not the same. There's a sort of biological imperative working here."

"I know. I know." Ronnie waved an impatient hand, as if genetics was just another one of those things that can be brushed aside by a determined woman. "I want you to pretend to be my sister."

I sighed. "Before I ask why you want me to do this, let me point out that we don't look the least bit alike. That might make this charade less than fully convincing."

At a couple of inches over five feet with a generously proportioned figured that any sighted male would call volup-

18

tuous, every molecule—indeed, every atom—of Ronnie's body was devoted to attracting men. Leave Ronnie alone for fifteen minutes in a locked room in a boarded-up building twenty miles away from any signs of civilization, and you would return to find her surrounded by a crowd of fawning males who would somehow have *seeped* into the building.

I was a couple of inches taller than Ronnie with slightly darker skin and brown curly hair. Although I was often called cute, with the praise occasionally reaching as high as pretty, I knew that I lacked a special something that Ronnie had.

"Pheromones. It must be pheromones," I muttered.

"Huh?" Ronnie said.

"Just thinking out loud."

"Well, we don't have to look much alike," Ronnie went on. "My oldest sister Molly is tall and skinny. She takes after my Aunt Isabel. You've seen a picture of her. She was married to my . . ."

"Why do you want us to pretend to be sisters?" I asked, interrupting our trip up and down Ronnie's family tree.

"I've met this guy at work."

I waited for her to continue, but Ronnie sat there with her eyes aglow, apparently believing that this simple statement provided enough reason for even the most outrageous request. Ronnie had a job in the service department of the local Lexus dealer. When she took the job, I had pointed out that she knew nothing about cars. She replied that no one expected her to actually fix anything; all she had to do was type, and not very long sentences at that.

"You meet new guys every day." Every minute, every second, heck, every nanosecond, I thought.

"This one is special. He's my Darling Everett."

"Your what?"

"His name is Everett Houser. But I call him Darling Everett."

Her eyes widened with emotion, reaching what must be the ophthalmologic limits for humans. "Of course, I haven't called him that to his face yet. But I think he's the one."

Finding THE ONE had been a monthly, if not semi-monthly, occurrence from the time when we first met as roommates during our freshman year at college. For the first semester I was continually afraid that Ronnie was going to drop out of college to get married. Only after several months had gone by did I discern the pattern that the current ONE usually had a lifespan of two weeks and begin to relax.

"How long have you known Darling . . . Everett Houser?"

"Since this morning."

"Ronnie, it is now one o'clock in the afternoon. Even by your standards, that does not make this a relationship of long duration. How can you possibly say that he's THE ONE?"

A baby-doll pout that men seem to find incredibly seductive came over Ronnie's face.

"Don't you believe in love at first sight?"

"I'm not even sure about second, third, or fourth sight," I said.

"Well, I do." She sighed, and her enlarged eyes took on a dreamy glow. "Maybe it was when he handed me the keys to his Lexus and said 'oil change and lube, please.' But I just knew. There was something in his voice."

"In his voice?" I tried repeating those words over and over in my mind but failed to find any romantic flavor in them.

"Well, maybe it was his eyes. The way he looked at me while I typed his order into the computer."

"Men always look at you."

"Then maybe it was when he asked me to the party tonight at his mansion."

"Mansion?"

"He called it a cottage. But when I asked him how large it

was, he said that it had ten bedrooms."

"Some cottage. Where is it?"

"Out in the Berkshires near Stockbridge. He drew a map for me."

"I remember hearing that back in the nineteenth century some of the rich families from New York City built summer places up here. They called them cottages because they were smaller than the mansions where they lived back in the city."

"Yeah. Everett did say something about this being a family summer home."

"So he invited you to a party. How does that make me your sister?"

"Well, I wanted you to come along. So I told him that my sister was staying with me, and I couldn't come if she didn't. It just wouldn't be polite."

"Why do you want me along?"

"I want to get your opinion of Everett."

Since Ronnie had never wanted my opinion of any of her other boyfriends, I decided this must be more serious than usual.

"And," Ronnie continued, "what if Darling Everett got busy showing people his collection of gold bars or something? Who would I talk to? I wouldn't know what to say to some trillionaire."

If it were a man, he wouldn't care what you said, he'd be happy just to look, I thought.

"But why did you say I was your sister? Why didn't you ask whether you could bring a friend?"

Ronnie held her leg out straight and flexed her foot so that the sandal made a raucous slapping sound.

"You know how I am. I always intend to tell the truth, but then a better idea comes into my mind. And before I know it I've told this . . ."

"Lie," I suggested.

"Story," Ronnie corrected. "I'm not trying to fool anybody, at least not about something important. And the made-up version just sounds so much better."

"Exactly what's the 'story' this time?"

"Well, it was just that I didn't want Darling Everett to think that I was afraid to be alone with him or anything. If I said I was bringing a friend, it would have sounded just so . . . medieval."

I was surprised that Ronnie knew the word, even though she had been a history major.

"So I told him about my poor spinster sister who's so lonely living out here so far from Boston. I said she would really love to have an opportunity to meet people of the opposite sex."

I made a sound in the back of my throat that caused Ronnie to look up in alarm.

"But I did tell him you were very pretty," Ronnie hurried on. "And I said that the only reason you couldn't get a guy was because you were a little reserved."

"Reserved?"

"Yeah, I think that's the word I used. Or maybe I said restrained."

"How about reticent or remote?"

"It was one of those 'R' words," Ronnie said, flapping her hand as if linguistic precision were an annoying gnat.

"So I'm supposed to be your very pretty spinster sister who can't find a guy because she's as frigid as a block of ice."

Ronnie nodded happily. "More or less. So will you come with me?"

She watched me with all the anticipation of a young child on Christmas morning.

"Sure," I said. "Why not?"

CHAPTER 4

Dear Auntie Mabel,

My parents divorced five years ago. I know they still love each other, and I very much want us to be a family again. Neither of them has remarried. Is there anything I can do to get them back together?

Despondent

Dear Despondent,

Sometimes we have to accept the bad things in life and move on. Your parents have been divorced for five years. They may still love each other, but this shows that they have chosen to live apart. I'm sure your parents love you, and in that sense you will always be a family.

Auntie Mabel

I pressed the button sending that one off to the editor, Sam Aaronson, and hoping you-know-who in the Farantello family happened to read the paper on the day the answer came out. I didn't like my chances. What kid reads the newspaper today?

I had come in to work in the middle of the afternoon to catch up on my column. I was also hoping to find someone to complain to about being nearly stoned to death, but no one was around. Even Mrs. Pear, the receptionist, had taken some personal time. This was frustrating because I've always found that talking about the bad things that happen to me makes them feel less overwhelming. Just as I was about to take another letter out of the Super Save More grocery bag I keep next to my desk to hold all my advising correspondence, the phone rang.

"So I guess you made a miraculous recovery from this morning?" Farantello asked when I picked up.

"Work waits for no man or woman," I said. "And an elastic bandage around the ankle does wonders." Ronnie had put it on for me and done a great job, even though the thought of Ronnie working as a nurse was a truly scary one.

"Yeah. I guess the same applies to parties. I called your house first, and Ronnie just couldn't wait to tell me that the two of you were going to some rich guy's house for a party tonight. I think she called him Darling Pervert."

"Everett," I corrected. "I'm going along to keep Ronnie out of trouble."

"Yeah, well, try to stay out of trouble yourself."

"It's not your place to say that to me anymore," I snapped.

There was a long silence. "You're right. I'm sorry."

"No problem," I replied, striving to sound less angry than I felt.

"Well, the officer who went to the property where the stone-thrower was located didn't find anyone. None of the neighbors were home except for one woman with kids who didn't see anything. I sent our civilian intern down to city hall to check the records, and she found out a Max Donovan owns the land. His application to build on the land has preliminary approval and should have final approval by the middle of next week."

"What's he planning to put there?"

"A house. I guess it's his own private dwelling."

"Does he live in town already?"

"No, I don't think so. His current home is in Boston. I called there but no one was at home. I got a number for the company he owns, also in Boston: Overlook Systems. I called there, too, and his secretary said he was away for several days. But she promised to call him on his confidential cell phone and have him get back to me."

"What does Overlook Systems do, keep an eye on people?"

"In a way. According to the Internet, they build satellite radar systems. I guess they've got a lot of government contracts."

"Well, I guess that's all you can do for now," I said.

"Yeah, if I don't hear from him today, I'll get on his secretary tomorrow and call his cell myself."

"Why would he want to build a home in Ravensford?"

"I wondered the same thing. His secretary said that he grew up out here."

"I shouldn't think a guy with a big business in Boston would want to live ninety miles away, even if it is his childhood hometown."

"Maybe it's meant to be more of a country place. Somewhere to unwind from the hustle and bustle of Boston."

"I can ask him about that when I talk to him. I might drive by the building site tomorrow and see if he shows up."

"I wouldn't advise that you go near his property again. Whoever threw stones at you last time might have improved his aim. I'll get in touch with Mr. Donovan, and when I talk to him, I'll discuss the assault on you."

"Make sure you let me know what happens."

Farantello agreed, then he said, "Well, have a good time tonight. Am I allowed to say that?"

"Of course, and I thank you for your good wishes. I'll be in touch."

The sun was creating a rosy glow in the west as I desperately consulted the back of the Lexus repair form on which Ronnie had hastily drawn a map to Everett's mansion. I finally realized that nothing looked right because north and south were reversed.

"Turn right here," I shouted, having finally flipped the map upside down in a sudden burst of enlightenment. I quickly grabbed the handle near the roof as Ronnie turned the Lexus on a dime and, with what sounded like some serious scraping of the undercarriage, bounced onto a private road.

When Ronnie first came out to live with me two months ago, never having owned a car in Boston, she borrowed my subcompact. Fortunately, within a few days of landing the job in the repair department of the Lexus dealer, the man in charge of finance was so smitten with her charms that he had gotten her a leasing deal on a new Lexus that could only be called criminal, and probably would be if the owners of the franchise ever found out. Ronnie's cowgirl style of driving made it doubtful whether the vehicle would survive the lease period.

"Take the next right," I said, giving Ronnie plenty of warning. "It's between those two pillars."

Advance notice didn't help. Ronnie maintained her Indy-500 speed, then wrestled the car to the right in such a way that all four wheels must have been off the ground at the same time. Barely missing the stone pillar on the left, the car hit the gravel road with the wheels still spinning and threw back a shower of stones that would have shattered the windshield of any car closely following us.

"Maybe we'd better slow down a little," I suggested. "You want to make a dignified entrance, don't you?"

My suggestion had an immediate effect. Ronnie slammed on the brakes, causing me to slide under the dashboard until my feet found the safety of the wheel housing. I pushed myself back up into the seat and tried to pull down the hem of my little black dress, which was now riding up to my hips. Meanwhile, Ronnie drove up to the top of the hill at a pace usually maintained by the lead car in a long funeral procession.

When we finally crested the hill, the view was breathtaking.

Directly in front of us was an expanse of green lawn that ran all the way down the hill to the woods. To the right we turned into a circular drive leading past a huge white building set on a little hill that looked more like a gracious hotel from the late nineteenth century than a private dwelling. With amoeba-like slowness Ronnie oozed us around the circle and stopped at the foot of a broad staircase that led up to the front door. A man who had been watching with increasingly obvious impatience as we made our leisurely way around the circle came down the steps to meet us.

I watched him approach. Tall, with broad shoulders and narrow hips, he was casually dressed in a knit shirt and khakis. In his early thirties, he looked a bit old for the typical valet. I wondered if he was a washed-up athlete from something-or-other sport working as a bodyguard for Everett Houser. A wealthy friend of mine once told me that the rich often like to employ the formerly famous in menial jobs.

"Oh, there's Darling Everett!" Ronnie shouted. Slamming the car into park, she bolted from the driver's seat, leaving the door open.

At first I thought she was referring to the man coming toward us, but Ronnie rushed past him without a glance and bounded up the stairs as fast as her tight skirt and four-inch heels would allow. I got out of the car and watched Ronnie rush up to a tall, very blond man standing by the front door. He was handsome in a sort of gentle, unformed way, like a very pretty child who has been enlarged. He saw Ronnie and his face transformed into a delightful smile.

The valet was watching them with rapt attention.

"You can park it anywhere," I said, holding out the keys. He stared at them as if they were a clutch of vipers.

"No, you can park it anywhere," he replied.

I turned to look at him. He had deep blue eyes, a slightly

unruly growth of thick brown hair, and a face that was just a shade too rugged to be called pretty. Handsome was the word, actually, but that was still no excuse for bad manners.

"You have an odd attitude for a valet," I said.

"If I were a valet, it would be; but since I am not, it makes perfectly good sense."

"What are you, then?" I sounded condescending even to myself, but rudeness in others always tends to get me up on my high horse.

"A friend of the host."

"And he has you parking cars? That's rather odd. You must not be a very good friend."

"I am not parking cars. The valet didn't show up. He probably had to work late at McDonald's, so I'm here to tell people where to park their cars."

The man took a step closer and studied me. I felt his gaze sweep over me like a pair of hands, and I was suddenly aware that the scooped neck of my dress was very low and the hem a bit too high.

"It's hard to believe," the man finally said.

"What's hard to believe?"

"That you are the spinster sister of that blond gold digger who's set on landing my best friend as her meal ticket."

I staggered back a step at the sudden insult, and my bad ankle turned on the gravel. The man reached over and seized me by the arm.

"Steady as she goes, princess."

"Take your hands off me," I said, sounding like the ingénue in a bad melodrama. I pulled my arm away.

"Fine," he said, releasing me. "The next time I'll let you fall on your butt."

"It would be better than being touched by you," I responded.

A smile came over the man's face. "I'm starting to see why

you're still single."

"I'm still single," I said, trying to make each word a sharp icicle that would penetrate his thick hide, "because so many men are like you."

"Now I'm hurt," he replied, pretending to pull an arrow from his chest. He glanced behind me. I turned and saw another car pull up behind ours. "Look, I'd like to stand here and exchange insults with you longer, princess, but you're holding up traffic. So why don't you take your car down to the lower lot," he said, pointing to a meadow on the other side of a hedge where several cars were already parked.

Without giving the man another glance, I turned and with as much dignity as I could manage in high heels on a gravel roadway, I walked to the driver's side of the Lexus. I drove very slowly around the circle to the parking area, so angry that I didn't trust myself to go any faster.

CHAPTER 5

Dear Auntie Mabel,

My son, Sam, has a good job with a landscaping company. He lives on his own in the spring and summer, but every winter he returns home to live with me because he isn't earning money. He doesn't pay me any rent and eats like a horse. Should I keep taking him in? He says that home is the only place where they can't say no.

Put-Upon Mom

Dear Put-Upon,

I suggest you tell Sam that home is one place where they can tell you to either get a full-time job or save your money for the winter. There is no reason you should support this hungry layabout. Tell him to pay rent or get a winter job and live on his own.

Auntie Mabel

I parked the car and sat behind the wheel staring straight ahead and breathing deeply, trying to regain my self-control. Running through my mind was a series of devastating replies I should have made to that infuriating man. Of course, I could march right back and say them now, but the moment had been lost. The cutting comeback loses some of its punch once the original remark is allowed to grow stale.

More than his crude remark about my unmarried state, what

bothered me was his comment about Ronnie being a gold digger. It might be true Ronnie lives by the motto that it's as easy to love a rich man as a poor one, but I knew she would never marry a man she didn't love. At least I didn't think she would.

Forget that appalling man, Auntie Mabel advised. *Get into a dispute with him and you will only sully yourself. She who slings mud gets dirty.*

I touched up my makeup in the vanity mirror, got out of the car and adjusted my dress, and began to pick my way up the gravel driveway. By the time I reached the stairway where the obnoxious man was still directing traffic, I had turned my heel twice and was thoroughly out of sorts.

"Didn't lock your keys in the car, did you, princess?" he said as I walked past.

Although under normal circumstances, I would probably have listened to Auntie Mabel, this time I snapped. I walked up to him. He pretended not to see me, staring down the drive as if waiting for the next car.

"Perhaps you could squeeze in an oil change for me while I'm at the party. Oh, that's right, I forgot, you're a friend of the host, so I'm sure you'll be too busy taking out the garbage once you're through here." I gave him a smile filled with false sweetness.

"Listen, lady . . ." he began, turning to face me.

"What's your name?" I asked. I had taken a small pad and a pen from my beaded bag and stood staring at him expectantly.

"My name?" he asked, confused.

"Yes, I'm sure you've got one, everybody does. I'd like to be able to tell Mr. Houser the identity of the person who has been announcing that one of his invited guests is a gold digger. I'm certain he'd like to be informed of that kind of thing."

31

"I'm Nick Manning," he answered slowly, a hint of worry on his face.

I asked him for the spelling and wrote it down on the pad with deliberate care. "And if not the valet, what are you really?"

"I already told you. I'm an old friend of Everett's."

"Sure you don't want to change your story? I'll ask Mr. Houser about it."

"Go right ahead," Manning said, seeming to regain some confidence. "And by the way, exactly who are you?"

"Laura Magee."

"Wait a minute. If your name is Magee, then why does your sister, who's single, have the last name of Blessington?"

I said a mental "oops" and gave myself a mental slap alongside the head. Ronnie should have known this ruse would never work. I've never been much good at lying. I lack the essential creativity.

"Ronnie isn't exactly my sister," I replied.

Nick Manning's eyes narrowed with suspicion. "What do you mean she's 'not exactly your sister'? I was standing right next to Everett at the car dealer's this morning because I was his ride. I distinctly heard the blond say that she wanted to invite her prim and proper single sister."

Prim and proper! I made a silent pledge that I would get even with Ronnie for this, but at the moment, it seemed essential to conceal how blatant a lie Ronnie had told.

"You must have misunderstood. Ronnie and I are sorority sisters, not biological sisters." Even that wasn't true. Neither of us had joined a sorority. I wasn't interested, and no sorority wanted Ronnie around stealing all the attractive men for herself.

"Sorority sisters!" Manning bellowed.

The disbelief in his voice was evident.

"Yes. A sorority is like a fraternity, only for women. You know what a fraternity is. It's where you drink your way through college while bragging about your athletic prowess."

"That stopped being a topic of conversation when I busted up my knee in my freshman year."

Now I felt a little bad, but not bad enough to apologize to this annoying man, who was now walking next to me as I made my way up to the house.

"Don't you have some traffic to direct?" I asked.

"Are you honestly trying to tell me that Ronnie goes around calling you her sister because of some sorority thing?"

"Sometimes Ronnie becomes a bit unfocused and fails to say exactly what she means."

"She's a liar. That's what you're saying."

Manning poked a finger in the direction of my face. I very much wanted to grab that annoying finger and bend it back to see how much pain he could withstand, but I decided that would be unladylike. A car pulled up at the bottom of the stairs.

"Shouldn't you be telling those people where to go rather than wasting time questioning me?"

"Pull it over there!" Manning shouted, pointing aggressively in the direction of the parking lot. The startled driver immediately pulled away, not giving his passengers a chance to disembark.

"Very charming," I said. "Are you by any chance a professional greeter?"

"I'm an architect."

"Really," I said, "I didn't imagine you in such a creative line of work. I thought you might be a bill collector."

I was being way more obnoxious than I usually am, especially to an attractive man. But I wasn't going to let him criticize Ronnie and get away with it.

"Look, Ms. Magee, if that's really your name. I'm not sure what kind of a game you and your big blue-eyed phony sister are up to, but Everett Houser is my best friend, and I have no intention of letting him be scammed by a couple of pretty con artists."

"Thank you for the compliment hidden somewhere beneath the insults. But I should inform you that I am an employee of the *Ravensford Chronicle* and Ronnie is, as you know, a customer service representative for Ravensford Lexus. We are both highly reputable people, and if you go around telling people otherwise, I will see that my attorney sues you for libel."

"Slander," Nick Manning said almost absentmindedly.

"Excuse me?"

"If I say the two of you are con artists and it's not true, then it's slander. If I write about it, it's libel."

"Really?"

He nodded his head.

I blushed. I don't like being wrong,

"Well, the point is, if you say or write anything false about us, I will see that you live to regret it."

Unexpectedly, he smiled. I felt a sharp pain in my chest as my heart skipped a beat. Smiles like that should be illegal. Dazzling white teeth, an adorable dimple in the left cheek, and a crinkling around eyes that I noticed could become greenish blue in the right light.

"Are you okay?" Nick asked.

"Of course, I'm fine. Why would you think otherwise?" I snapped.

"You had a slightly dazed look."

"That's my normal look. Now why don't you go back to doing your job?"

He stared hard at me instead. "Look, I don't care what you think of me. Just remember that Everett has been my friend for a long time, and nothing bad is going to happen to him if I can prevent it."

I glanced up at the large house and said in a gentler voice. "It seems to me that a man who has all of this should be able to take care of himself."

Manning's expression softened slightly. "You might think so, but Everett inherited all of this after his parents died in the crash of their private plane when he was ten. He was raised by his grandmother, but she left the real work to a series of nannies hired to supervise Everett's education and development. They were more accustomed to taking care of small children, and as he grew older, they treated him as a sort of large-sized little boy. Until he went away to college, his life was pretty limited."

"But surely by now?"

Nick shrugged. "He's smart enough. When it comes to handling his business empire, he can even be quite shrewd, but in his personal life, he's pretty gullible. In many ways he's still that ten-year-old boy who's been left all alone and who very much wants to be liked."

"So when you saw Ronnie take such an immediate interest in Everett, you were afraid that he would end up being hurt."

"It's happened before," Nick said. "Money and good looks are a combination that attracts lots of women, and many of them are motivated more by self-interest than by affection."

"So have you taken the place of Everett's nannies? Do you follow him around and investigate every woman he takes an interest in?"

He shook his head slowly. "We've been friends since college, but I have my own life and Everett has his. He works out of offices in Boston now, and I'm in Springfield, so we only get together when he's in the western part of Massachusetts. But we talk on the phone several times a month. I try to give him advice, but when there's some pretty thing making eyes at him, my influence is limited. So far I've managed to keep him from marrying any of these gold diggers, but I'm not sure how long my luck will hold."

"Well, I can assure you that Ronnie, whatever her weaknesses, would not marry anyone just for their money."

His eyes locked onto mine. "I'll make my own decision about that."

I was getting a bit tired of Nick's protective friend routine. Two could play that game.

"As Ronnie's closest friend, I have real doubts about whether Everett is suitable for her."

"He's a great guy," Nick said, suddenly on the defensive.

"He sounds like an emotional cripple to me. I wouldn't want Ronnie to spend the rest of her life babysitting a husband who has all the maturity of an adolescent."

Nick's face hardened. "Maybe you shouldn't be so quick to judge somebody you don't know."

"You formed a pretty fast opinion of Ronnie."

"I know the type."

I opened my mouth to respond, then thought better of it. There was nothing to be gained by arguing with this infuriating, narrow-minded man who could only see in Ronnie the stereotypical blond bombshell on the make. I turned and walked away, relieved and slightly disappointed that this time he didn't follow me.

CHAPTER 6

Dear Auntie Mabel,

My boyfriend likes to take pictures of me in the nude. This makes me extremely uncomfortable, although he says that it gets him hot. I might be willing to put up with this, except I think he is showing the pictures around to his friends because lately I've noticed that some of his male friends are looking at me differently. What should I do?

Double Exposed

Dear Double,

If your boyfriend's shutterbug tendencies make you uncomfortable, you should ask him to stop in no uncertain terms. If he is showing the photos to his friends, the next stop might be posting them on the Internet, where there is no telling who might see them. This is a clear invasion of your privacy. The pictures he has already taken, along with the microchip or negative originals, should be returned to you, so that you can determine their disposition. If he refuses to do this, I would tell him to hit the road and take a picture of my door on the way out.

Auntie Mabel

I made my way up the stairs and into the house. I went through a spacious lobby and down a wide hallway to my left. Eventually I found myself in a large, mostly unfurnished room filled with people talking and eating. One wall was made up of a series of French doors open to a wide veranda that provided a beautiful view of the surrounding fields. But by this time I was more interested in the large buffet table running the length of the inside wall. I decided I'd look for Ronnie to warn her about Nick Manning after I'd had something to eat to build up my strength.

I took a plate and quickly filled it with various salads and breads. Full plate in one hand and diet soda in the other, I made a quick survey of the room and saw no empty chairs. The crowded veranda outside the French doors didn't seem any more promising. Determined to sit down so that I could truly enjoy my food, I headed back out into the hall the way I had come. Not feeling that it was polite to open closed doors, I went past the lobby and into the opposite wing of the house before I came across a partially opened door. Shoving the door open with one foot while I balanced on the other, one of the few valuable moves I'd learned from my time at Live Like a Tree yoga studio, I saw what appeared to be a study. There was a desk in one corner, an easy chair in the other, and a large sofa and several wing-backed chairs arranged in front of a fireplace. Better yet, the room was empty. The drapes were pulled, but a lamp on one end table cast a gentle glow over the creamy white walls.

The door is open and the light is on, I reasoned. That makes it fair game for a hungry girl to use as a resting place. I didn't want to be seen clearly from the doorway by a wandering guest who might decide to join me, so I selected the easy chair in the dark corner and began to eat. Twenty minutes later, feeling much fuller and more relaxed, I leaned back in the plush chair and fell asleep.

My eyes snapped open. I didn't know why, but I must have heard something. Moving my head as little as possible I scanned the room, sensing rather than seeing another person. Suddenly a head popped up from behind one of the wing back chairs near the fireplace. A short, thin man, dressed all in black, walked over to stare at the painting over the mantel.

A cat burglar, I thought, and certainly a brazen one to contemplate stealing art in the middle of a party. Then I saw, as he stepped further into the light, that the man was not dressed for second story work but was merely wearing what passed for party clothes among those people overly influenced by Hollywood: a black sport coat, black slacks, and black shirt. I'd seen plenty of those outfits when I'd worked in Boston.

Feeling more confident, I stood up. "Hello," I said.

The man whirled around and clutched his chest, simultaneously giving a short cry of distress. I would have been more concerned if he had been grabbing his left side rather than his right, but it was still a very fine performance.

"Oh, but you surprised me," he gasped in an accent that sounded like it came from somewhere in Europe to the east of France.

He appeared to be in his early thirties; thin, mousey brown hair barely covered the top of his head, and a wispy goatee clung to his chin. About two inches shorter than my five-five, he looked up at me with something close to awe.

"Sorry, I didn't mean to frighten you," I said.

"It is nothing. I did not know that I was sharing the room with such charming company. But please excuse me. I should introduce myself. I am Sebastian."

After he said Sebastian, all I could make out was a throat clearing sound.

"Excuse me," I said after I had introduced myself, "But could you spell your last name?"

"Most gladly. K-r-a-n-k."

"Crank," I suggested.

The man flinched. "It is pronounced more or less to sound the same as your wild horse."

Mustang passed through my mind, but there was no way I could massage k-r-a-n-k into that.

Sebastian held imaginary reins and made a bucking motion with his scrawny rear end. The light dawned.

"You mean it rhymes with 'bronc,' " I said.

"Precisely," he said with a pleased smile. He sank down on the sofa and patted the seat next to him. "Won't you join with me for a moment?"

Despite the somewhat ambiguous term "join with," there was a certain desperate friendliness about the man that I found appealing. I sat down next to him.

"If you will excuse me for saying so, a woman as beautiful as yourself must be a model."

"I'm not, but thank you for the compliment. By the way, my name is Laura Magee."

"May I ask, then, what do you do for a living?"

"I work on a newspaper. The *Ravensford Chronicle*."

His admiring glance was replaced by one of barely suppressed excitement.

"Do you ever write any articles about art?"

"Well, I haven't, not for the newspaper. But I used to work for a Boston art museum, and I've written about art."

Like a man who's been wandering in the desert for days and suddenly sees a lake of cold beer, Krank's eyes widened as he bounced up and down on the sofa cushion.

"What a marvelous coincidence," he exclaimed, reaching over to take my hand as if I had just accepted his proposal of marriage. "I happen to be an artist."

I'd seen that coming way down the road, and I gently but firmly disengaged my hand.

"Really," I said.

Back in Boston, I had often found myself being hit on at parties by men who were more enamored of my job than of me.

"Would your newspaper be interested in writing an article about the show of my sculpture that is about to open at the Ravensford College gallery?"

I was about to put him off with a noncommittal reply when I thought, why not? This was something I could do, and it would give me a whole new area of work in journalism aside from being Auntie Mabel and doing the occasional investigative story.

"That's a good idea," I said.

"I am also an American citizen," he said proudly.

"Good for you."

"Krank! What are you doing here?"

Nick Manning stood in the doorway leaning forward aggressively, as if all that restrained him from attacking the little man was an invisible leash. Behind him a couple turned to stare, trying to see what could have made him so irate. I wondered myself.

"Well, isn't this cozy? The princess and the pauper," Nick said. "Now the thieves are conspiring together."

This man is very impolite, Auntie Mabel said. *He really should be more careful in his use of accusatory language.* I couldn't agree more.

"You seem to see thieves everywhere. Did you ever consider that you might have a streak of paranoia?" I said.

"No, because I happen to be surrounded by real thieves," he said, glaring at me.

"I have already told you what I do for a living, and Mr. Krank was just telling me that he's a sculptor."

"So's my uncle Ernie. He makes swans out of ice."

"And he is also a citizen of the United States," I continued.

"Of course, Uncle Ernie is a citizen."

"I was referring to Mr. Krank."

Nick laughed as though the very idea was absurd.

"I am from the west," Sebastian said, lifting his chin and trying to appear defiant, but only managing to resemble an irritated schnauzer.

"Where? West Berlin?" asked Nick.

"My parents were living in California at the time I was born. They returned to Austria when I was ten months old. Being born in this country makes me a citizen."

"Citizen or not, you weren't invited to this party," Nick said, stepping toward Krank, who leapt to his feet, whether to fight or run was hard to tell.

I stepped between Nick and the little man.

"Don't be such a bully," I said.

"I'm not," Nick protested, clearly stung by my remark. "But Mr. Krank has been hanging around here trying to sell sculptures to Everett for the last week, and he's been very insistent. Waiting in the bushes outside the door to waylay Everett when he arrives, and even attempting to get into the house by claiming to be a vacuum cleaner salesman."

"A noble American profession," Sebastian added, making sure to remain out of Manning's reach.

I turned to the artist. "But not your profession."

"Indeed, not. I am a sculptor," he piped up proudly.

"And have you done all of these things Mr. Manning has accused you of doing?"

Sebastian bowed his head and extended his hands toward me in a pleading gesture.

"Please, Laura, surely you understand. A poor artist must do what he must to become recognized."

I knew that I could own a newspaper of my own if I had a nickel for every time I'd heard that justification for bad behavior back in Boston.

"Perhaps you should leave now, Sebastian. It sounds as if Mr. Manning has some reason for being harsh."

"Harsh!" Nick sputtered. I raised a hand directing him to be quiet. Surprisingly, my imperious gesture worked.

I turned back to Sebastian whose face had taken forlorn to new depths of meaning. I thought for a moment that he was going to burst into tears.

"Do you have any portable examples of your work available?"

He gave me a puzzled look. "Do you mean that fold up?"

"No. I mean do you have any that are small enough for you to personally carry to the newspaper?"

He nodded happily.

"Then select the best one and come to see me at the newspaper tomorrow around two o'clock. I can't promise anything, but I will arrange for the acting manager of the *Chronicle* to take a look at it."

Sebastian reached out and startled me by grabbing my right hand and pressing it fervently to his lips.

"Thank you, dear Laura. I promise that you will not regret this decision you have made to give a young artist an opportunity."

"Better have him bring his birth certificate, too," Nick added dryly. "That sounds as creative as his sculpture."

Waving farewell to me several times and giving Nick a wide berth, Sebastian left the room.

"I wouldn't have figured you for a soft touch," Nick said.

"Have you actually seen his work?"

Nick glared at me for a moment. Then he smiled and shook his head.

"I guess you're right. I try to keep guys like Sebastian away from Everett because Everett feels sorry for them and before long he's paid twenty thousand for a giant painting some guy did with a squeegee. How about we leave the job to you of deciding whether Krank gets to see Everett? If you think his work is good, I'll suggest that Everett take a look at it."

Clever move, Manning, I thought. Not only had he acted pleasant and reasonable, but he had shifted the job of being the heavy to my shoulders. Now I really had to make a serious judgment of Sebastian's work, because a wealthy patron would be depending on it.

The couple standing in the doorway behind Nick must have decided that nothing more was going to happen because the man stepped into the room and cleared his throat impatiently in an attempt to get Nick's attention. He was in his early fifties, handsome in a well-groomed and carefully maintained sort of way. The woman next to him was clearly twenty years younger, tall and thin as a model, attractive enough to make her casual sundress look the height of fashion.

"If you're through here, Manning, my wife and I would like to get back to the party."

The man paused and gave me a slow, detailed onceover. Rather creepy, especially since his wife was there to watch him do it.

A flicker of distaste passed over Nick's face as he turned to the man.

"Sorry to keep you waiting." He turned to me. "Laura Magee, I'd like you to meet Victoria and Max Donovan."

The name rang a bell, but for the moment I couldn't recall where I'd heard it before.

Max took my hand and held onto it a bit longer than necessary. His wife kept smiling and pretending not to notice her husband's grabby ways.

"I enjoyed watching you give my architect here a hard time. Usually that's my job." Max followed up with a laugh intended to soften the comment, but it didn't quite work. Nick stared at him, stony faced.

"Are you building in this area?" I asked. "It certainly is beautiful."

"Not exactly," the man said. "We're building in Ravensford. I grew up there and still have some family out this way. My wife

44

convinced me that a retreat within two hours of the city would be a good idea. With the stock market being the way it is, I decided we'd be smart to put some money into real estate and have a place of our own to stay for our visits."

"I see. Where are you building?" I asked as the nickel dropped.

"Right on the hill overlooking the Ravensford River. We were lucky we got the last piece of land along there that you can build on."

"Really! Well, someone was standing on that piece of land and throwing rocks at me this morning," I said. "Would he be following your orders?"

Max's smile disappeared. "We've had some trouble with the neighbors. Folks coming around and bothering the work crew. Finally, I had to take a guy who worked security for me back at the office and post him out there. I told him to approach people coming on the land and ask them why they were there. If they didn't have a good reason, he was to tell them that they were trespassing and escort them off the property."

"Well, he's taken to throwing rocks first and asking questions later. And I wasn't even on the property. I was just walking up the hill from the river."

Donovan shook his head and smiled, not seeming very disturbed by what had happened. "I'll have a talk with Merv. He can get a little overly enthusiastic at times."

Victoria Donovan nodded her head in agreement and her nose wrinkled as though Merv was not her favorite person.

"What's his full name?" I asked, taking a small notebook and a pen out of my purse."

"Merv Tilson. But don't worry. It won't happen again."

"I've already reported the incident to the police, so they'll probably want to talk with you and Merv."

Max frowned. "I'm sorry that it's gone so far already. I'll stop by the police station on my way through town and explain everything. Were you hurt?"

"He hit me a couple of times, and I sprained my ankle getting away." I held my foot out so they could see the compression bandage.

"I told you . . ." Victoria Donovan began, but Max's glance silenced her.

"Please send me a bill for any medical costs, and I hope your ankle is better soon."

I nodded.

"Nick and I will be out there tomorrow morning around ten, walking the property so he can show me exactly where everything will be. If you could find the time, maybe you'd like to stop by and see what the place is going to look like. Since nothing has been done yet beyond some clearing of trees and bushes, you'll have to use your imagination to picture the final result, but I'll bring a set of plans."

"I'd like that," I replied. I figured it might be a way to meet my attacker. Also I wanted to find out more about Nick Manning in case he turned out to be a problem for Ronnie.

"It's the least I can do."

I thought it was, as well.

"That's great," Max said, turning to his wife, who gave a bland nod. "Well, let's get back to the party."

Nick walked next to me as Max and his wife moved on ahead.

"If your schedule is too tight tomorrow and you can't make it, Max and I will understand."

I smiled. "I can feel my schedule loosening up as we speak."

"What I mean is, you don't have to bother about tomorrow. Max can be a bit overbearing at times, and there really isn't much of interest to see. It might be a lot of slogging through mud and fighting off bugs. There might even be snakes."

"Nice try, Nick," I hissed in his ear, making a sound similar, I hoped, to that of an irritated rattler. "But I have every intention of getting a firsthand impression of what this house is going to look like. What style would you say it is?"

Nick sighed. "I began with a plan for a small, one-story structure that snuggled right into the slope. Most of the back would be glass, so they'd have a great view out over the river. But Max wanted a house like the ones they saw on their trip to Burgundy. So he kept adding on and adding on, so it's slowly morphed into a chalet of over five thousand square feet."

"In other words, a real blight on the landscape."

"Maybe not quite that bad, but not what I would have liked."

"What kind of an architect are you? Do you let your clients tell you what kind of house to build?"

"Well, yeah. This isn't like being an artist where you do the painting, then try to sell it. With architecture, you have to come up with a plan that pleases the client or else the house never makes it off the drawing board."

"Even if that client is a philistine whose bloated, unsightly house will ruin the neighborhood?"

"That's a bit of an exaggeration," Nick said without conviction.

I snorted. "Let's face it, Manning, you are nothing but an architectural . . . whore."

"Whore?" Nick said, his face turning red.

"Exactly. You're willing to sell your services to anyone who will pay the price."

I knew I was over the top. I knew I was being unfair. But I was tired, my ankle hurt, and Nick had repeatedly gotten on my nerves; so instead of apologizing, I spun on my heel and went click-clacking down the hall to the front door, making even my footsteps sound angry.

CHAPTER 7

Dear Auntie Mabel,

The daughter of a friend of mine is getting married in a month, and her sister is giving her a bridal shower next week. The bride and groom have been living together in their own house for five years, so they already have all the normal items that would serve as gifts. Frankly, I think they have a lot of nerve having a shower at all, so my question is do I have to give them a gift?

Unsure

Dear Unsure,

Like most things in life, if you want to play the game, you've got to pay the price. If you want to go to the shower, instead of engaging in a silent protest by not attending, you must bring a gift. To do any less would be tacky.

Auntie Mabel

Before I got halfway down the hall a hand grabbed my arm and turned me around.

"Leave me alone," I said when I saw it was Nick Manning. I pulled my arm away. "I don't want to talk to you."

"Well, I don't want to talk to you either, but we've got a problem."

"What?"

Nick nodded at a tall, distinguished gray-haired man wearing a black suit.

"Apparently Mr. Everett has disappeared," the man said in a discreet whisper.

"Who are you?" I asked.

"I am Williams, the Houser family butler."

"How do you know he's disappeared?"

"I have searched all the rooms and the veranda with no success."

"Maybe he's in the bathroom off of the master bedroom. Didn't he get locked in there one time when the doorknob came off?" asked Nick.

"That has been fixed, sir. But I have already checked that bathroom just in case there was a reoccurrence."

"What does any of this have to do with me?" I cut in. I was learning far too much about the day-to-day life of the Houser family.

Nick nodded once again to Williams.

"He was last seen in the company of Ms. Blessington."

Several choice comments about Ronnie flitted through my mind, but I kept them to myself.

"Are any of Everett's cars missing from the garage?" asked Nick.

"They are still on the premises."

"Then probably Mr. Houser and Ms. Blessington are as well."

"Perhaps they left in Ms. Blessington's car, sir."

"Not possible, Williams," I snapped. "I have the keys to the car."

"Is there a second set?" Nick asked.

"I don't know," I admitted

"Do you both have cell phones? Can you call her?"

"I left mine in the car."

Nick shook his head as if to say that I was useless. "Williams, why don't you walk through the garden to the folly and see if anyone is there."

"What would they . . . ?" Williams stopped and his face took on a slightly roguish expression. "Do you think Mr. Houser and Ms. Blessington might be canoodling in the folly?" he asked.

"We can't ignore the possibility. Perhaps you can make a certain amount of intentional noise in the course of the search to serve as a warning of your approach. That might help to avoid embarrassment."

"Of course, sir. I could sing one of the sea shanties I learned in my youth."

"Good. Ms. Reynolds and I will check on Ms. Blessington's car."

Williams nodded and went down the main hall toward the door, already humming a nautical air.

"I knew your friend would be trouble," Nick said to me.

"You can't blame them for wanting to spend some time together."

"This is Everett's party. He shouldn't be hiding from his guests."

"Aren't you the stuffy one," I said, although secretly I agreed with him, and I knew Auntie Mabel would, too.

The parking lot had filled up since I arrived, and it took us a few minutes to locate Ronnie's Lexus. I finally spotted it at the end of a row. As we walked toward it, I pushed the remote to unlock the doors. By the glow of the interior light we saw two figures jumping around inside the car as if they were sardines making a desperate last-minute escape before canning.

"We must have surprised them," Nick muttered. "Too bad you didn't push the emergency button."

I walked closer just in time to have the rear door fly open, almost hitting me in the side.

"Oops! Sorry! Excuse me!" a tall, blond-haired man mumbled, while he struggled to rearrange his clothes. Ronnie slid out next and quickly smoothed down her skirt.

"Hi, Laura," she said, as calm as ever.

"Sorry to disturb you," Nick said with heavy sarcasm. "We couldn't find Everett anywhere, and we got concerned."

"No problem," Ronnie said. She turned to me and said, "I'd like you to meet Everett Houser."

"Hi," he said, sticking out his hand in a doubtful sort of way, like someone who isn't quite sure how to behave around adults.

I smiled and reached in the direction of his hand but barely brushed it. I wasn't about to make greater contact under the circumstances without wearing a rubber glove.

"Um, sorry about being hard to find and all," Everett said. "We were . . . um . . ."

"Getting acquainted. I understand," I said.

"Well, I don't," Nick said. "Jeez, Everett, there are ten bedrooms in that house. Couldn't you have found somewhere less public than the back seat of a car?"

"It isn't just a car, it's a Lexus," said Ronnie, suddenly the automotive professional.

Nick turned to her, looking for a hint of sarcasm, but found nothing but sincerity. He gave his head a bewildered shake.

"I guess there are ten bedrooms," Everett said, as though it was something he'd never fully considered. "But I knew that as soon as I went missing, Williams would begin searching every room in the house."

"He did, then he came looking for me. You're lucky he found me or he'd have been on the phone to the FBI to report a kidnapping."

"Sometimes you guys go too far," Everett said with a petulant frown.

I half expected him to stamp his foot or hold his breath until he turned red. I could see that Nick was right. His friend was clearly a case of arrested emotional development. The mind of a boy trapped in the body of a rather handsome man worth many millions of dollars. It was hard to know whether the mind would ever grow into the body, but I had my doubts whether Nick's protective approach, however understandable, was the right way to go about it. Most likely it just encouraged Everett's immaturity.

"I think I'd like to go now," I said. "Are you ready?"

"I guess," Ronnie reluctantly agreed.

"I'll drive," I said, hoping to avoid the problems we'd encountered on the trip in.

"You'll call me tomorrow, won't you?" Ronnie asked, moving closer to Everett.

"Sure, I will, pumpkin."

She wrapped her arms around his neck and in an instant their lips were locked together. Nick and I stared at them in embarrassment as the kiss continued. Finally, I managed to wedge an arm around Ronnie's waist and pull her away from Everett.

"Time to come up for air, kids, and head home."

Ronnie disengaged and we got into the car. Nick stood close to Everett's side as if afraid he might attempt to stow away in the trunk.

"Good night, sweetie," Everett called as I carefully backed the car out and began to pull away.

"Good night, Darling Everett," Ronnie called back.

I glanced at Nick as we went past the two men, but he refused to meet my eye. I was surprised to find that I was disappointed.

"It looks like you and Everett hit it off pretty well," I said once we were on the main road heading home.

"Hmm."

When nothing more was forthcoming, I glanced over at her in amazement. Ronnie usually had to be restrained from chattering on endlessly about her dates, whether good or bad. By the light of the dashboard, I could barely make out the expression or lack of one on her face. Her normally animated features were relaxed. Although it was not a word that I would normally have associated with Ronnie, I had to admit she appeared serene.

"Are you all right?" I asked.

"Hmm."

"You didn't take any drugs at that party, did you?"

"No."

"Then 'hmm' does not constitute an acceptable response. Was Everett Houser everything you expected him to be?"

Finally, Ronnie turned in her seat to face me. "Nothing like. I thought he would be this charming, in command, confident sort of guy."

"And he's not like that at all?"

"Not a bit of it. He's shy, kind of bumbling, insecure, and really worried about whether people like him. He's like that nerdy guy in high school who asked me to go with him to the prom."

"Did you go?" I asked.

"Of course not. But now I wish I had."

"Because he turned out to be a computer whiz worth a hundred million?" I asked.

Ronnie stared at me, puzzled. "No. He runs a hardware store back in the town where I grew up."

I sighed. Talking with Ronnie sometimes made me feel like a rat that has just been plunked down in a particularly frustrating maze. I scrambled to backtrack to the beginning of our conversation.

"So you were saying that you like Everett because he's a nerd, and you wish you had gone out with more nerds in the past."

"It hit me like a ton of bricks," Ronnie said, losing me again.

"What did?"

"Here I've been searching around for the kind of man I

thought I wanted: handsome, rich, and self-confident. And now I've discovered that I only want the first two." Her voice took on the emotion of someone speaking eternal truths when she said, "I've discovered that what I really want is a handsome, rich, immature guy."

"Are you sure that's . . . wise?" I asked.

Ronnie nodded hard enough to make all her curls bounce at once.

"I had, like, this moment of self-revelation tonight. What would a self-confident, secure guy want with me?"

I gave her a sidelong look.

"Aside from that," Ronnie said with a grin. "After all, I'm not like you. I'm not sophisticated or polished. You can dress me up in a business suit, but no one is ever going to mistake me for an executive type. I've only got two things going for me aside from my looks: I'm nice and I'm loyal to the people I care about."

"And you think that's what Everett needs?"

"Absolutely. He isn't stupid. It's just that no one has ever taught him the kinds of things he needs to know to be a man. Oh, Nick has tried, but there are some things a woman is just better equipped to do."

"This nurturing side of yours is surprising," I said. "Most women save that aspect of themselves for raising a family, not bringing up their husbands. You talk about Everett like he's your little boy."

"Only in some ways. In others he is definitely a man."

"So I gathered from that little ballet in the car. But whatever Everett may think of you, Manning isn't your friend."

I filled her in on what had happened back at the party.

"So be careful. Manning may try to turn Everett against you."

"Everett has a mind of his own," Ronnie replied.

I let that go. "And by the way, I don't appreciate being

presented as your pathetic, spinster sister who needs a pity date."

"A little pity never hurts. Look what it got you. You're seeing Nick again tomorrow. Maybe he'll ask you out."

"And why would I want to go out with the Desecrator of the Vandersnooten Memorial?"

Ronnie gave me a quizzical look, so I filled her in on my meeting with Max Donovan.

"Manning has no moral fiber or he would never have consented to put up the eyesore Donovan proposed," I concluded.

"But I want you to like Nick," Ronnie said, crossing her arms and adopting a stubborn expression.

"Why does it matter?"

"Because when Everett and I get married, I want you to be my maid of honor, and I'm sure Everett will want Nick to be his best man. It would spoil my wedding if you and Nick were fighting through the whole thing."

"If, and let me point out it is still a big *if*, you and Everett should marry, I am certain that Manning and I will be adult enough to behave appropriately." If we survive the rehearsal dinner, I added to myself.

"But what about the future of my children?"

"The what?" I was tempted to stop the car because I clearly couldn't follow the conversation and drive at the same time.

"Well, it's obvious, isn't it? You and Nick will be the godparents of our firstborn and probably will be responsible for the whole lot of them if anything terrible should happen to both Everett and me, heaven forbid. The two of you have to be friends if you're going to share a responsibility like that."

"I see. Under such tragic circumstances, I suppose we could work together up to a point. Perhaps we could be associates rather than friends."

Ronnie sniffed. "I'm not sure I could entrust the future of my young children to people who were merely 'associates.' "

I pulled into the driveway of Grandmother's house. We went inside and upstairs to our bedrooms.

I was about to close my bedroom door when I felt the need to say more.

"Just one word of advice. If Everett is really as immature as you say he is, take it slow. You've got to give each other time to find out if a relationship is going to work."

"One day at a time," Ronnie said gaily.

"Right idea. Wrong problem."

"Okay. But you have to promise me that you and Nick will at least try to be friends."

"I promise that I'll give him every opportunity to see things my way."

Ronnie smiled and nodded.

"Hey, that's not what I mean," she called out a few beats too late, after my bedroom door had closed.

CHAPTER 8

Dear Auntie Mabel,

I recently discovered that my husband has been going to bars and telling other women that he's a widower. And all the times he told me he had to work late or he would lose his job, he's been having dates with sympathetic girlfriends. How can I put an end to this disgusting deception?

Outraged

Dear Outraged,

Tell your husband that you are wise to his little scheme and if he doesn't start coming home right after work, your marriage will be over. Either you'll divorce him or you'll honestly be able to go to bars and tell men that you are a widow.

Auntie Mabel

The next morning I parked my car in its customary spot in the newspaper parking lot, right in the shade of a large oak tree on the edge of the asphalt, where it would stay cool even if the afternoon turned warm. As I walked into the office, I said good morning to Mrs. Pear. She returned the greeting and smiled at me, showing a set of nicotine-stained dentures. Dorie Lamont, the college student who had manned that post part time for a couple of years, had given up the job to focus on school. Since she had supposedly spent the last five years as a full-time college student and only achieved the status of sophomore, her mother demanded that she either concentrate on her schoolwork or get a real job. That was enough motivation for Dorie to at least pretend to be a serious student.

Mrs. Pear, a widow of indeterminate age, had been a personal choice of Roger St. Claire, the newspaper's owner. All he would say regarding her qualifications is that she used to be his favorite waitress in a coffee shop he went to as a much younger man.

I dropped off my bag at my desk and took a quick right turn down the corridor that led to the acting general manager's office. Along with hiring Mrs. Pear, St. Clair had also hired a replacement for himself while he was whiling away his time on the beach in Florida with my grandmother. Again he went for somebody from his past by hiring Walter Rumson, who had been in his class at Amherst College close to sixty years before.

Wally had been a curator of ancient Middle Eastern art at the Metropolitan Museum of Art in New York until his forced retirement two years ago. Bored out of his mind with retirement, he contacted his friend Roger at just the right time, and St. Clair had provided him with a temporary job. Although Roger St. Clair was a very hands-on owner and general manager, he clearly had told Wally not to interfere in the daily running of the newspaper. In fact, he must have warned Wally not to do much of anything except hang out in his office, because that was all he did. Hang out and pursue his hobbies.

My knock on Wally's door brought a grunt that might have been interpreted as "come in." Anyway, I chose to interpret it that way and opened the door. Wally was in a corner of the office hunched over a table that had a small vise attached to it. A bright fluorescent desk lamp glowed down on something clamped in the vise.

"Come and look at this, Laura," Wally said, not even glancing behind him to see who had come into the office. I don't know how he did that. I asked him once and he said that in the cut-throat world of curating, you always had to know who was coming up behind you.

I did as he asked and peered over his shoulder at what appeared to be a clump of feathers and trinkets tied together with nylon thread.

"An ancient tribal fetish, sir?" I asked, knowing very well what it was.

Wally smiled at my little joke. "A sheep nose," he announced.

"Ah," I said, trying to put the proper amount of appreciation into my tone.

When Wally moved from Manhattan to western Massachusetts, he believed himself to be relocating to the most primitive of locations. An area where he thought he might well have to be able to catch and kill his own food. Even though he had never put a hook in the water in his entire life, Wally became enamored with the idea of fly fishing. Many lessons and thousands of dollars of equipment later, the only part of fly fishing that still appealed to him was making his own flies, of which he now had a huge and ever-growing collection.

The fact that none of his flies was in any danger of touching water unless some splashed on them from the carafe on Wally's desk made no difference. Standing thigh deep in a cold stream while hoping not to catch pneumonia or slip on a rock and drown held no appeal for Wally, although he continued to deceive himself and others by talking as if fishing would be the goal of his next vacation. But I think all of us knew that for Wally, tying flies was an end in itself.

"It's very difficult to make," Wally said, defensive at my lack of appreciation.

"It's certainly a very odd name for a fly. Why would a trout or bass or whatever you were trying to catch want to take a bite out of a sheep's nose? I suppose sheep might sometimes drink out of streams and could fall victim to a vicious fish, so perhaps that's where it came from."

Wally sighed then smiled. "You're looking particularly lovely this morning. The color of that shirt is perfect with your eyes."

I thanked him. Since I was wearing jeans and an old shirt because of my planned tour of a construction site, I knew he was flattering me. What might have constituted sexual harassment from another boss, however, seemed like a genuine compliment from a man old enough to be my grandfather, but who still had a sprightly twinkle in his blue eyes when he talked to women.

"I'm sure you're not here just to fish for compliments, or out of any interest in fishing," he said, glancing down sadly at his sheep nose.

"Actually, I would like to have your decision on something."

He frowned. "If it has anything to do with running the paper, you should probably talk to Sam Aaronson or call Roger in Florida."

"I need someone who knows something about art."

He grinned boyishly. "Then I'm your man."

He swiveled his chair around and motioned for me to sit down across from him. Wally never sat behind his desk. Maybe he thought that spot really belonged to Roger.

"I have an artist dropping by this afternoon. I told him that if we liked his work, the newspaper would cover his exhibit up at the college."

"If he's still alive, I doubt his work will appeal to me."

"I know your field of specialization is ancient Middle Eastern art and, as you always say, it's a long and winding road from ancient Mesopotamia to contemporary Massachusetts, but I'd appreciate it if you would give me your opinion of this guy's sculptures. He's coming in at two o'clock today with an example of his work. If you think it has some merit, I'd like to do a review."

Fortunately, Wally didn't ask me why, if I thought myself

capable of writing a review, I needed his opinion. The real reason was that Sam Aaronson probably wouldn't approve the project unless I had Wally's backing.

"At two o'clock I'll be at your disposal," Wally said with a generous wave of his hand. "But let me warn you, I will be applying a high level of aesthetic standards."

I looked down at the sheep nose still firmly clamped on the bench looking like a small, colorful, but dead animal.

"I'm sure you will, sir," I replied.

I studied the map of Ravensford I'd borrowed from the office and turned down a street named Rivers Edge, which looked as if it would take me to the construction site. Sure enough, it was a road running parallel to the river with houses on either side. On my left, the properties apparently ran all the way back to the bank of the river. This had to be the neighborhood I was looking for, and sure enough, four blocks along I came to a construction site on my left. Two cars were already parked along the road in front. I added mine to the line.

I began walking over the ground that had already been scraped clear of vegetation, leaving bare dirt. All that remained was a small forest of trees along the back by the river. I saw Nick Manning and Max Donovan standing on one side of the lot consulting over what appeared to be a set of plans. Max saw me and waved that I should join them.

"We'll put the tower at this end of the roofline," I heard Max say as I drew closer.

"Tower?" Nick asked, a puzzled frown wrinkling his forehead. "There was no tower in the original plans."

"But you can draw one in, right?" Max said with a definiteness that bordered on command.

"You're building a private residence, Max, not a castle," Nick said with a nervous smile, clearly hoping this was all a very unfunny joke.

"Is there some law of architecture that says you can't put a tower on a home?" The man's face had instantly tightened, and his jaw stuck out belligerently.

"There's no law. But I don't think a tower will look good there."

"I don't care how it looks. It's the view that counts. I want to put my study at the top of a tower where I can look right down on the river once I've had some of those trees cleared away."

"We're going for a modern colonial look, so for the sake of symmetry we really should put a tower on the other end to balance it out."

"That's going to cost a lot more money, and it won't give me anything I don't already have."

"Wouldn't your wife like a tower study with a view?" Nick asked.

"All she needs is a fancy kitchen to impress her friends," Donovan said. "Anyway, she doesn't care what the place looks like as long as it's in Ravensford. This was all her idea to begin with."

"Well, the house will look better with two towers. That means when you sell you'll make more money."

A slow smile spread over Donovan's face at the mention of money. "I knew there was a reason I hired an architect instead of designing this place myself."

You mean aside from your complete lack of competence, I thought. I could tell by the expression on Nick's face that he was thinking the same thing.

"But how much are two towers actually going to add to the price?"

"I'll have to check with Doug," Nick said, taking out his cell phone.

There was a wooden sign stuck in the ground at the front of

the property with Doug Alsop's name on it as the general contractor. Doug was best known around Ravensford for putting up economy condominiums, and I figured Max had chosen him for his willingness to work cheap. I wondered if Doug would be as horrified as Nick at the prospect of building a mini-castle. From what I'd heard of Doug, he probably wouldn't care as long as he got paid.

I didn't want to have to make small talk with Donovan while Nick was on the phone, so I wandered to the end of the property along the riverside where the trees and bushes remained untouched. Since I had on my grubby clothes, I decided to walk through the bordering woods and see whether the view of the river was as great as Max thought. I pushed my way between a couple of tall bushes and into the small forest. I was crunching through the leaves and broken branches that gave the ground a bouncy thickness when I gracelessly stumbled over a large stone and fell to one knee. I stood carefully, testing my bad ankle, which I'd fortunately had the foresight to wrap once more in an elastic bandage.

As I stood there trying to decide how my ankle felt, I saw a bright shade of blue behind a small tree to my right. Since blue is a relatively rare color for vegetation, I walked over to take a look. At first I thought it was just a piece of cloth that had blown into the woods and gotten stuck in the foliage, but as I came closer I could see that it was large and oddly shaped. When I walked closer still, I saw a body. I stopped in my tracks, my heart racing. Then I walked a little nearer. The face was turned away from me, so I walked around the body in a wide circle. I didn't want to startle some homeless person sleeping in the woods.

But when I saw the face, I knew this guy wasn't sleeping.

CHAPTER 9

Dear Auntie Mabel,

My sister-in-law says the most insulting things to me then quickly says, "only kidding," as if that makes everything all right. I've complained to my husband about this, and he says she's always been this way and that it's just part of her quirky humor. Maybe so, but I don't find it very funny. It's also ruining my relationship with my husband's family. What can I do to get her to stop?

Insulted

Dear Insulted,

You could have a heart-to-heart talk with your sister-in-law, telling her that her "humorous" comments are hurtful to you. If that doesn't work, the next time she insults you, reply by saying "I think you're a horse's ass," then smile sweetly and say, "only kidding."

Auntie Mabel

I struggled to make myself understood to Nick and Donovan. The words seemed to come out all jumbled, but I must have eventually been clear enough, because they immediately ran off into the woods in the direction I had come from. I felt a little shaky and sat down on a tree stump.

When they returned, looking grim, Nick said, "It's Merv Tilson. We'd better call the police right away," and he took out his cell phone.

"Just a minute," Donovan ordered.

There was a long pause as Nick and I stood there frozen, watching Donovan. It was probably the shock setting in, but for one clear moment, it seemed that I could read his mind. He didn't want a body found on his building site, because that would lead to even more complications with building his house. He was sorely tempted to have Nick take the body's legs while he took the arms, and they'd carry old Merv like a used carpet to another location and dump him there. Maybe they'd just roll him down the bank toward the river. Who knew when the body would be discovered? By then it wouldn't be his problem. But what if they were seen? Moving a body was probably some kind of a crime, and moving the body of your own security person might be an even worse one. Plus, Donovan wasn't sure that he could depend on me to keep quiet or on Nick to help him.

Even a bad man will sometimes do the right thing out of prudence, Auntie Mabel whispered in my mind.

This time she was right.

"Yeah," Donovan said, "we've got to call the police."

While Nick was making the call, I said to Donovan, "How do you think he died?"

"There's blood all over his face. Looks like he hit his head somehow."

"Was he supposed to be out here this morning?"

Donovan shook his head. "I talked to him last night and told him that after what he did to you yesterday, he should stay off the site until further notice. I even let him know that his job was in jeopardy."

"Was there any sign that he was here when you arrived this morning?"

Donovan shook his head.

"What did he drive?"

"A Ford pickup. But there was no sign of it when Nick and I got here."

Before I could ask him any other questions, Donovan pulled out his cell phone and walked away.

"Are you all right?" Nick had finished his call and was standing next to me. His eyes showed genuine concern.

"I'm okay. It was just a shock."

He nodded.

"How did you happen to go out there?" he asked.

"I wanted to see what the river looked like from the top of the slope. I wonder what Tilson was doing out there."

"Maybe he was checking to see if anyone was walking up the slope from the river like you did yesterday. He might have been planning to give him the same reception." Nick paused then went on more quickly, "That could be what happened. He started throwing stones at someone, and either the person threw one back that hit him or sneaked up the slope behind him and did him in."

"Donovan said he told Tilson not to come out here anymore."

Nick shrugged. "The few times I met Tilson, he didn't strike me as the kind of guy who took orders really well."

"Could it have been an accident? Maybe he tripped and fell and hit his head on a rock."

"It had to have been a very hard fall. And I didn't see any large rocks right near his head. Did you?"

"No, but I can't say that I looked around carefully," I admitted.

"And if it was an accident, what happened to his truck?"

Before I could say more, a patrol car pulled up in front of the building site. An unmarked car parked right behind it, and Farantello got out. I saw him pause slightly when he saw me, then he continued walking until he was standing right in front of Nick and me.

"I gather you found a body out in the woods," he said, alternating his stare between the two of us.

"I did. I mean I found it first," I said.

An "I should have known" expression quickly passed over Farantello's face.

"Do you want to take me to the body?"

"I'll do it," Nick volunteered.

"And you are?"

"Nick Manning. I'm the architect for the house being built here."

"And you've looked at the body, too."

Nick nodded.

"Who else has tromped around the crime site?"

"He has," I said, nodding in the direction of Donovan, who was shouting at someone on the phone.

"Ah, wonderful," Farantello said. "And who is he?"

"Max Donovan. He owns this land and is planning to build a house on it," Nick answered.

Farantello nodded, "I talked to him last night about that rock-throwing incident." He fixed his stare on Nick. "Why don't you show me this body? And by the way, does anyone know who he is?"

"Merv Tilson." I said.

"That's the guy Donovan said threw the rocks at you."

"I guess he is. I never got a good look at him, but he was wearing a blue coat and so is the dead man."

"You never actually met Tilson after the rock-throwing incident?" Farantello asked me.

"No," I said emphatically, suddenly feeling like I was a suspect.

Farantello just nodded, then motioned for Nick to lead the way.

"Don't go anywhere," he said to me. I would have been worried, but he gave me a little smile. Of course, maybe he smiled at everyone before he slapped on the cuffs.

As soon as Farantello and Nick were out of hearing range, I took out my cell phone and called the paper. I wanted to alert Smitty, the guy who did most of our photography. This would be worth the trip. He wouldn't be allowed to photograph the body, not that it would serve any purpose, since the newspaper wouldn't print it, but he could always take a picture of the empty lot. We could run that over a caption: "Man's Body Found." For some reason a picture always added to the story, even when it didn't convey any information.

I wandered around the site waiting for Smitty to arrive. There wasn't much to see. From what little I knew about construction, after the land was cleared, the next step would be to dig out a hole for the cellar and foundation. Aside from some cigarette butts and a small pile of chewing gum wrappers behind a bush in one corner of the lot, there wasn't much to see, so I was kind of relieved when Smitty's pickup truck pulled up in front of the site and his long, thin frame unfolded from behind the driver's seat.

"What've you got?" he asked me with an eager smile.

"A dead male back there," I said, pointing to the woods. "Apparently he was sort of a security guard for the site."

"An accident?" Smitty asked. He was trying to be realistic since the odds of murder in Ravensford were pretty slim, but I could hear the hope in his voice.

"Don't know yet, but it sure looks suspicious. Farantello is out there right now."

"He won't want me walking around much. I think I'll just take a few shots of the area so we'll have something to use with the story."

A few minutes later Farantello and Nick came back across the lot. They were walking side by side but not talking. It could have been a companionable silence, but I doubted it.

"So what do you think happened?" I asked Farantello.

"I can't be sure, since I didn't want to disturb the body before the state crime scene guys get here. But it looks to me like he was hit on the top of the head."

"So nobody threw a rock at him."

"That might have been poetic justice, but the angle isn't right. He might have been struck on the head with a rock by somebody taller than he was, but unless somebody dropped it out of a tree onto his head, the rock wasn't thrown."

"So it probably wasn't an accident either," I said.

Farantello shook his head. "But don't quote me on that. Not just yet."

Farantello spotted Smitty, who was taking a picture of the sign with the name of Doug Alsop's construction company on it. I didn't think Doug would appreciate the publicity, but maybe he believed in the old saying that any publicity is good publicity.

"He knows better than to try taking a picture of the body, right?" Farantello asked me.

I nodded. "Can I leave now?"

"I don't see why not. I have a copy of your fingerprints on file. I'll give them to the state boys. I know where to find you if I have any questions," he answered, and I thought I saw a twinkle of humor in his eye. "Since you were at the crime scene, you'll have to wait to be fingerprinted," he said to Nick.

"What the hell are you doing here?" Donovan roared. He had finally stopped shouting into his phone and had spotted Smitty. "I'll have you arrested for trespassing."

Smitty gave him an amused smile. The kind you might flash at a tiny dog that was trying to appear large by barking loudly. Donovan looked like he was about to rush at Smitty and give him a body bump, but Farantello quickly got between them.

"I'm going to have to ask you some questions," he said to

Donovan. Then he turned to Smitty, "Are you about done here?"

"Sure am," Smitty replied amiably.

Smitty and I strolled back to the street together.

"Get all the pictures you needed?" I asked.

"More than enough."

"It looks like a murder."

Smitty's smile broadened. "Think that type-A guy back there did it."

"I'm sure he'll be in the running."

"Probably didn't do it, though."

"Why not?"

Smitty took the camera off his neck and stowed it in a bag behind the front seat.

"He's making too much noise. If you had just killed somebody, would you want to attract all that attention to yourself?"

I thought about it.

He has a very good point there, Auntie Mabel said.

"You're probably right," I replied.

CHAPTER 10

Dear Auntie Mabel,

Some of my buddies and I get together regularly to hoist a few in our local watering hole. All of us buy a round except for Slim who always has to leave just before it's his turn. Slim is a lot of fun to have around, but we're getting tired of his cheap ways. None of us has a lot of money, so everybody has to chip in. What should we do?

Sucked Dry

Dear Sucked Dry,

I would suggest that when it comes time to buy the second round, somebody says to Slim, in a friendly but firm voice, "How 'bout it partner, are you ready to buy?" If Slim doesn't take the hint, then replace him with somebody who has a keener sense of fairness.

Auntie Mabel

Back at the office I checked in with Sam Aaronson, our managing editor, and got the go-ahead to write the story on Tilson. Russ Jones usually does most of the stories on local news events, but it wasn't unheard of for someone else to cover a story if they happened to be on the scene or if Russ wasn't available.

Russ used to be an anchor on one of the big Boston television stations until he accidentally made an X-rated comment about the weather girl in front of what turned out to be a live mike. Women's rights activists joined with defenders of the children to get him removed from his position. St. Clair hired him because Russ's grandfather had been a friend of his. Although we had all waited with bated breath to see if Russ was even semi-literate, writing not always being a requirement for television anchors, we were pleased to discover that he actually wrote well. He even seemed pleased to be working in a medium where you pretty much knew when your words were going to become public. As far as his attitude toward women, he hadn't yet tried to harass me. I didn't know whether to be offended or relieved.

Two hours later I had finally honed my article into good enough shape that I was willing to subject it to Sam Aaronson's critical eye. As I returned to my desk, getting ready to delve into my bag of Auntie Mabel questions, I saw Sebastian Krank looking warily across the front counter at Mrs. Pear. I checked my watch. It was two o'clock, time for our appointment with Wally.

"So why are you dressed all in black? Are you one of them Goths or something?" Mrs. Pear asked, giving him a critical inspection.

"No, Madam," Sebastian replied, drawing himself up to his full five-feet-three. "I am not a Goth or a Vandal, and only a very rude person would call me a Hun."

"Then why are you wearing black?" she asked, pointing at him with a tobacco-stained finger.

"I am not wearing black."

She snorted. "Mr. Pear always told me that I had the best vision of any woman he knew."

Sebastian's eyes took on a panicky expression, as though he was now certain that this elderly woman accosting him was in a cartoon world of her own and would soon be making references to Mr. Apple and Mr. Orange. Then his eyes fell on her nametag that was partially concealed by the collar of her striking, lime green jacket.

"Ah," he said with a smile of relief. "Mr. Pear is your husband."

"Was. A fine man, too. But now I'm in the market for my next. I think I'll try for someone a little younger this time," Mrs. Pear said with what she no doubt thought was a beguiling smile that made her dentures flop loosely.

Sebastian backed away from the desk as if expecting her to reach over at any minute with her thin arms and clutch him to her shrunken bosom.

"Anyway, I know black when I see it," she concluded with a challenging stare.

Sebastian pulled a handkerchief out of his pocket and draped it over the sleeve of his coat.

"Observe. The handkerchief is pure black, while my coat has a gray thread running through it."

Mrs. Pear pushed her glasses up and leaned so far across the counter to study his arm that she became alarmingly red in the face. I decided that in the interest of employee safety, it was time for me to bring this conversation to a close. I stepped up to the counter next to her.

"I do see!" Mrs. Pear exclaimed. "You're right. The handkerchief is a shade darker." Then a glint of shrewdness entered her eye. "But maybe that means your coat is just a lighter shade of black."

Sebastian shook his head firmly. "There are no degrees of black. It is the ultimate in darkness."

Mrs. Pear spotted me. "The fella is right. He's not dressed in black."

"Charcoal gray," I ventured.

"Precisely," Sebastian said, delighted. He beamed at me and grabbed my hand, pressing it to his lips.

"Only one thing still bothers me," said Mrs. Pear. "Why

would a man carry around a black handkerchief? It doesn't seem quite natural, you know?"

Sebastian smiled. "It is a statement of my nihilism, a symbol of the ultimate meaninglessness of life."

Mrs. Pear slowly moved her dentures up and down for a moment. "I figured it was just because it would always look clean."

"Did you bring something for me to look at?" I interjected before Sebastian could respond with an explanation of his personal philosophy.

"Indeed, fair lady." He snatched a paper bag off Mrs. Pear's desk. Reaching inside he made an elaborate show of removing something. "Voilà!" he said, opening his hand to reveal a small wooden sculpture.

"May I?" I asked. Sebastian nodded excitedly as I removed the sculpture from his hand.

At first I thought it was purely abstract. The curves were smooth under my hands, and the entire piece somehow seemed to fit in my grasp as if it had been fashioned just for me. A sense of peace and serenity flowed through me as I held the sculpture. Only as I began to examine it in detail did the figure become recognizable as a bear. Once I saw it that way, it seemed inconceivable that I had ever missed its representational quality.

"Why, it's a bear," I said.

"It is made from mahogany," Sebastian said, looking on like a proud parent. "I've done a number of bear forms recently. This is my smallest. I am in my bear period, so to speak."

"Doesn't look like any bear I've ever seen," Mrs. Pear said, pursing her lips as if she'd just tasted a lemon. "And I can tell you, Mr. Pear used to be quite the hunter in his time. And that was when bears were bears."

Sebastian turned to her with a small, confident smile. I could see that in the place of the strange, nervous man was an assured artist.

"The point, Mrs. Pear, is not to create a sculpture that looks like a bear, but to create a sculpture that will change how you look at bears."

Mrs. Pear lapsed into a rare moment of silence and chewed on her dentures thoughtfully.

"It's wonderful," I said, reluctantly handing it back to Sebastian, who returned it to the bag. "We have to show it to our general manager, Walter Rumson."

Sebastian nodded and followed me down the hall to Wally's office. Just as I knocked on the door there was a crash inside, followed by a loud oath.

"Perhaps this is not a good time," Sebastian said nervously.

"Nonsense, this happens all the time."

"Come in! Come in!" a voice called from inside.

I cautiously pushed open the door, wondering what disaster I would find. Walter was standing behind his desk, fly rod in hand, and glaring across the room at a lamp lying on the floor amidst the shattered remains of its glass shade. On the floor in front of the shelf on which the lamp had once rested was a bowl that I recognized Walter used as his fly-casting target.

"Another Tiffany bites the dust," I said. "Maybe you shouldn't be doing that in here."

"A lamp by Louis Comfort Tiffany," Sebastian said in a reverential tone, gazing down on the colorful shards of glass as if they were the remains of his best friend.

"Just a cheap knock-off, old man," Walter said heartily, coming around his desk and seizing Krank's limp hand in his own. "We buy them by the bushel load."

"We have to," I added.

"Why they don't have places for indoor fly casting, I just can't understand," Wally said, glancing to Sebastian for support. "There's indoor tennis, why not indoor fly casting?"

He stared hard at Krank, clearly waiting for a reply. The artist licked his lips nervously. I decided to help him out.

"Perhaps because being out in the great world of nature where there are real fish is an essential part of true fly fishing."

Wally waved his hand dismissively. "The point of fly fishing isn't to catch fish. It's to make lures and learn how to cast. Fish are an unnecessary distraction."

"A lot like lamps," I suggested.

Wally ignored me. "So you're the sculptor?" he said, giving Sebastian a cheery pat on the back that made him cringe. Krank looked at me with eyes that pleaded for some help in handling this madman.

"He's brought a small sample of his work that I think you might like to see."

I nodded at Sebastian, encouraging him to open the bag and take out the bear sculpture. The artist seemed a bit uncertain as to whether he wanted to show his work or run. Finally, pride won, and he took out the small statue. It sat in the palm of the hand he extended toward Wally. I heard a sharp intake of breath and knew that Wally shared my opinion. He gently took it in his left hand and fumbled for his reading glasses in his right. When they were on his face, he carefully studied the small statue.

After a few moments he glanced up and his magnified eyes stared into mine. "Why, it's positively Assyrian!" he exclaimed.

Sebastian seemed about to object, so I broke in, "Indeed it is, sir."

I knew that for Wally, Assyrian was the highest praise. He caressed the bear, smiling broadly.

"Marvelous. Absolutely bloody marvelous," Wally said, lapsing into Briticisms that remained from his years in London. As he gently fondled the statue, a troubled look came over his face. "But a piece this size. It would not have a very effective presence when put on display."

"I have an identical figure in a larger size on display at the college." Sebastian indicated with his hands something about three feet long and two feet high.

"In wood?" asked Wally.

"The one on display at the college is in wood, but I have also done it in marble. That piece is back at my studio. This is a design that I am very fond of."

"Have you done other animals?"

"A frog and a turtle."

"Wonderful."

I would have found Wally's enthusiasm mystifying if I didn't know that he loved the sculptures of animals done by the Assyrians.

"So I can do a piece on Sebastian's exhibition at Ravensford College?"

"Of course, certainly," Wally said distractedly.

Sebastian reached out and seized his hand and began shaking it forcefully.

"Easy there," Wally said, pulling back his hand. "That's my casting hand."

"Sorry," Sebastian said, looking stricken.

"Do you have an agent?" Wally asked.

Sebastian shook his head.

"Well, I think you'd better get one, because I'm going to call my friend Jack Hitchings at the Hitchings' Gallery down in Manhattan. I'm going to strongly suggest that he start carrying some of your work."

Sebastian's eyes grew wide and he started breathing so heavily, I thought he was going to hyperventilate. Before I had to resort to a paper bag, however, he calmed down. He reached out and grabbed Wally's hand one more time and pumped it up and down.

"You will never regret this," Sebastian said fervently.

Wally retrieved his hand, stretching his fingers as if he regretted it already.

"I'm sure I won't," Wally said, taking a step away from Sebastian, who was once again eyeing his hand.

"You'll see that your confidence has not been misplaced."

Wally picked up his rod, clearly anxious to get back to his indoor casting.

"Do you have a card? I'll let you know what I hear from Hitchings."

Sebastian handed Wally a business card, then appeared ready to launch into another round of thanks, so I gently began guiding him to the door and out into the hall.

"This is wonderful," Sebastian said to me, then his face turned cautious. "But Mr. Rumson seems to me to be a somewhat eccentric person."

"Some would say that," I agreed.

"Can I be sure that he is completely serious in what he says about my work?"

"Wally never lies or even sugar-coats his opinion about art. And if he promises to do something to see that your art is marketed, I am certain he will do it."

A relieved smile settled on Sebastian's face. He threw his arms around me and gave me a huge hug.

"This is the happiest day of my life. Please let me show my appreciation by taking you out to dinner."

"Thank you for the invitation," I began, getting ready to turn him down gently.

"Hey, you, where do you think you're going?" Mrs. Pear shouted from the front desk where she'd been studying a tabloid as usual. She hopped out of her chair, ready to apprehend the interloper, saw that it was Ronnie and, shaking her head, she settled back down in her chair.

"Laura! I just have to talk to you," Ronnie said, rushing up to me, her round face flushed and her blond curls bouncing as if they had a life of their own.

I gave her a stern look to indicate that a business meeting was in progress. "Ronnie, I'd like you to meet Sebastian Krank. Sebastian, this is Ronnie Blessington."

"Enchanted," Sebastian said, grabbing Ronnie's hand and pressing it to his lips.

"Me, too," Ronnie replied, snatching her hand away fast enough to give Sebastian's lips rug burn. "Laura, you just have to come to dinner with Everett and me tonight."

"Why?"

Ronnie gave a petulant little wiggle that I considered childish, but from the sudden fascination on Sebastian's face, it must have been infinitely seductive to a man.

"You just have to," she repeated. "We've invited Nick, and he agreed to come only if you were there. He said, 'Be sure to invite your spinster sister.' "

"Oh, that's what he said, is it?" I felt a dull heat rising from my neck to my face.

"That was very rude," Sebastian said, his face becoming stern. He turned to me. "Would you like me to settle his hash?"

I smiled doubtfully, not sure whether to take Sebastian seriously. All I could picture was a Chihuahua attacking a Great Dane. I decided to play it safe.

"No, thank you. But I do appreciate the thought."

"So you will come, won't you?" Ronnie urged.

"Only on one condition."

"Anything," Ronnie said.

"Mr. Krank has just invited me to dinner tonight. I will be very happy to join you and Everett if Sebastian can be my escort."

Ronnie's smile dipped slightly. "You'll have to promise not to shoot Nick," she said to Sebastian, her blue eyes taking on a pleading quality no healthy man could resist. "That would absolutely spoil everything."

Sebastian gave a brief bow. "I will do my best to control my hot Austrian blood."

"Six o'clock at Johnson's," Ronnie said, "Everett likes to dine early."

Much against Sebastian's gentlemanly instincts, I insisted on meeting him at the restaurant rather than being picked up, and I quickly got rid of both him and Ronnie by saying I had some urgent work to complete. As I watched Sebastian and Ronnie go down the walk to the parking lot chatting happily, I sighed once again at the ease with which Ronnie was instantly able to find the common biological denominator in all men. But I sighed more deeply at the thought of tonight's dinner. Why would Ronnie and Everett insist on having Nick and me there? Did they have an important announcement to make? The very thought made me nervous—so nervous, in fact, that I jumped at the sound of another crashing lamp coming from Wally's office.

CHAPTER 11

Dear Auntie Mabel,

I work for a small company and generally enjoy my job. Recently, however, due to the poor economy, the salaries of all the employees have been cut. At the same time the owner of the business has taken several expensive vacations and purchased a luxury car. Morale in the office is very low, and people are working less because they resent the owner's behavior, feeling that it is not equitable in the present economy. I am concerned because if the company goes out of business, I will have a difficult time getting another job.

Worried About Job

Dear Worried,

Many people will suggest that you and several other loyal employees talk to the owner privately about your concerns. That will sometimes work. However, your employer seems to be tone deaf when it comes to the feelings of his employees, so he may simply decide to fire all of you. I suggest that you either suck it up until the economy improves or else send an anonymous note pointing out to him the negative consequences of his actions. That may frighten him into behaving better. I would also start looking for a new job.

Auntie Mabel

I punched the button that sent my column off to Sam Aaronson for final editing before being sent to layout. I leaned back in my chair and looked across the room. Mrs. Pear's chair was empty, but through the window I could see her around back having a smoke and chatting with the printing crew. Since Sebastian had left an hour ago, I'd done my normal Auntie Mabel duties, but in the back of my mind, I was thinking about the apparent murder of Merv Tilson. I had written the first story about the murder, although at Sam's insistence I hadn't come right out and called it a murder, referring to it instead as a "suspicious death." There was no guarantee that I'd be assigned to follow it up. I was primarily Auntie Mabel, not a crime reporter. Finding the Vandersnooten memorial and checking on a building lot were about the extent of my investigatory duties. I wandered down the hall to where Sam was sitting in his small office wearing his visor and peering through heavy glasses at today's stories as they marched by on the computer screen.

"Should I write a follow-up on the Tilson story for tomorrow?" I asked.

"Is there anything left to say?" Sam asked without looking up.

"I don't know yet."

"Do you want to find out or should I put Russ on it?"

I was so surprised he'd asked me, that I was silent for a moment. My silence must have unnerved Sam because he added, "Just thought you might like a change of pace."

For a guy who tossed words around as if they were made of gold, this was the height of conversational extravagance.

"Sure, I'll look into it."

"Get me something for tomorrow's paper. That means I want it on my desk by eight in the morning at the latest."

I went back to my desk and thought about how I should proceed. I could call Farantello and find out if he had learned anything new, but I was reluctant to do that for several reasons. For one, I doubted he would tell me anything really important because he wouldn't want to make public a truly promising lead. Also he would be accountable to the state investigator who would be in charge. Another reason was that I didn't feel like being so reliant on a guy who had recently dumped me. Finally, I had a sort of naive view that a reporter should go right to the source, and in this case the best source of information seemed to me to be the owners of the properties bordering the Donovan site. Maybe I'd be duplicating what the police had already done, but there's nothing like getting the story firsthand.

After telling Mrs. Pear where I was going, I drove out of the center of town and went the quick half-mile to where Donovan was building his tacky estate. It was right around lunchtime, so I figured that anyone who didn't have to go to a job in town would probably be around.

I started with the Cape Cod directly across the street from the building site, figuring its owners would have had the best view. I rang the bell. No one came to the door right away, but I could hear sounds from the back of the house. Crying interspersed with shouts to stop crying. I rang the bell again, figuring that persistence might pay off. Finally, the door opened and a woman no older than I stood there. She was wearing jeans and a gray shirt that had stretched out at the waistband. In one arm she held a baby, and attached to her other hand and screaming as if he were being tortured, was a boy that I guessed to be around two. She bent down and said something to the boy that caused him to become quiet, but by the expression on his face, I could tell he would be starting up again at any moment.

She opened the door about a foot and said, "I already have my own religion."

I nodded at that interesting but completely irrelevant piece of information, then it clicked with me that she thought I was a holy lady looking for converts.

"I'm Laura Magee. I work for the *Ravensford Chronicle*. I just wanted to ask you a few questions with regard to the body found across the street."

She shivered slightly and gave me a thin smile. "I'm Jennifer Boyce. Nice to meet you. But I'm afraid I've already told the police everything I know. And I don't want to be in the paper." She reached up and tried to push her hair back into place, which made me wonder if she was adverse to publicity or only to publicity that made her look bad.

"I only have a few questions, and I won't quote you."

She nodded but continued to appear doubtful.

"Yesterday morning did you see anyone on the construction site?"

"We don't spend much time in the front of the house because the family room and the boys' bedrooms are in the back. But around ten-thirty I always put them down for a nap and try to read the newspaper. Then I usually sit in the front room. I looked over there around then and saw three cars and some people checking things out."

That was when Nick, Donovan, and I were there. I needed somebody who had been watching the place earlier, when Tilson arrived. Of course I didn't know whether he had arrived early that morning or during the night. I'd have to ask Farantello if the medical examiner had any idea as to the time of death.

"Is there anyone who might be keeping a closer eye on the neighborhood?"

She laughed. "You mean closer than a mother with two small kids? Yeah, Frank Taylor. I think that must be all he does. He's retired and a one-man neighborhood watch. He sent around a petition for us to sign, asking the town to block construction on the site."

"Did you sign?"

"Sure. I always thought of that vacant lot as a place where

my boys could play when they got older. But then Frank wanted us to picket the site. He said we'd get lots of publicity, and that might be enough to get the town council to reexamine the application for a building permit. Can you see me on a picket line with two children?"

"Where does this guy live?"

She pointed to the house on the left side of the building lot.

"Frank used to treat that wooded area by the side of his house as if it were part of his own yard. He put out bird feeders and seed for the squirrels. I think he even had a picnic table under the trees that was there until the contractor cleared them away."

"It's too late to get his little forest back."

"I know. Now I think what Frank wants is revenge. He'll do anything he can to block the building of that house."

"Sounds like a guy I should talk to."

"I'm sure he'd be happy to be interviewed if there's a chance of getting some publicity."

The two-year-old began pulling on her hand and making the same kind of sound I feel like making at a party when I'm bored. I figured any moment he'd take a deep breath and break into full howl.

"Do you have any children?" the woman asked me.

I shook my head.

"Lucky you," she said, then immediately seemed shocked at her own comment.

I glanced down at the boy to see if he had understood, and whether this was going to harm his tender psyche. But he was completely focused on catching a bug climbing up the screen.

"I didn't mean that the way it sounded," Jennifer said. "It's just that being home alone with the boys all day, sometimes I feel that life is passing me by. I hardly ever see another adult, except for twice a week when I take them to their play group."

"I can imagine that must be hard," I said.

She nodded. The boy began pulling on her arm, so I quickly thanked Jennifer and headed back down the walk. Before I reached the street, I could hear a high keening sound of discontent.

I suspected I'd be hearing a similar sound of unhappiness but in a lower register as I walked up to the front door of Frank Taylor's house. He must be the "Concerned Frank" who had written to Auntie Mabel, but I couldn't let him know, or my secret identity would be exposed.

The door opened before I took my finger off the bell, so I figured that he'd been watching me when I talked to Jennifer. He was a round guy; one of those who has more in the middle than necessary but carries it well. His head was bald in the middle with a fringe of gray hair around the edges, but his brown eyes had the alert look of someone who didn't miss much.

"Can I help you?" he asked matter-of-factly.

I told him who I was and explained that Jennifer had referred me to him. He quickly pushed open the aluminum storm door and stepped back so I could enter the house. Off to the immediate left was the living room. I settled into an occasional chair in front of the picture window. The seat was still warm, so I suspected that this was one of Frank's favorite observation posts.

"I knew something bad was going to happen," Taylor said before I could ask a question.

"Why?"

"Well, it stands to reason. You start tearing out nature just so that you can put up an ugly house. That's just asking for trouble."

"How did you know it was going to be an ugly house?"

"No house was going to be as pretty as those woods were," he said. "And I talked to Doug Alsop one day when he was checking things out. I've known Doug ever since he was a boy, and from what he told me, I knew it was going to be one of those tasteless cookie-cutter pseudo-mansions people are putting up all over."

You don't know the half of it, I thought to myself. Wait until you see the towers.

"Did you see Merv Tilson on the site early yesterday morning or maybe the night before?"

Frank shook his head. "And I sure would have noticed that creep's truck."

"Why do you call him a creep?"

"The guy tried to hit me, and I was just practicing my Constitutional right to free speech and assembly."

"Would this be your picketing campaign?"

He nodded. "I got Jerry and Kay to join me, and we just walked in the street in front of the site. We called your newspaper. Somebody said he'd come out, but he never showed."

He waited for me to respond, as if I was supposed to offer an explanation for any failing of the *Chronicle*.

"I have no idea why they didn't follow up on your call. I'll ask back at the office."

He waved an indifferent hand as if he were accustomed to getting the same runaround everywhere he went.

"So what happened when you picketed?" I asked to move things along.

"This was back when Doug and his crew were just starting to clear the land. I talked to Doug, and he said the owner of the property wasn't there, but he had all the proper permits to start work."

"What did you do then?"

"We just started walking up and down carrying signs that said 'Save the Trees,' 'Preserve Access to the River,' and 'Stop Overdevelopment.' "

"And what happened?" I asked.

"Nothing until this Merv Tilson shows up in his truck. He hops out and starts telling us that we'd all better get out of there. He was shouting and acting like a wild man. Jerry and Kay got so scared they walked half a block away, but I stood up to him and said that I had every right to be in the street right where I was."

"What did Merv say to that?"

"He didn't say anything. He pushed me. I almost fell down. I think he would have pushed me again when this other guy who was talking to Alsop walked over. I found out later that he's the architect. Well, he got between us. Merv was so mad that he even pushed him, but this guy pushed Merv right back, and he fell down. It might have turned into quite a ruckus, but just then Kay called over that she'd phoned the police. Tilson got back in his truck and beat it out of there."

"What about the architect?"

"He hung around and talked to the patrolman who finally showed up."

"And this was when?"

"Five days ago."

"Is there anyone else living around here who keeps an eye on the site?"

"Sure, there's Kay. She's got the calmest head amongst all of us."

"And where does she live?"

"Her house is right on the other side of the work site."

I stood up, ready to make my way to Kay's. "What about Jerry, the man who was with you at the protest demonstration? Should I visit him?"

"Jerry Waxman. His house is half a block away. He was there mostly to show his support for his friends. He wouldn't know who was at the work site."

I nodded.

"Is any of this going to get into the paper?" Frank asked.

"There was a story about the murder in today's edition," I said, a little hurt that he hadn't noticed my byline.

"The kid doesn't bring my paper until late in the afternoon," Frank explained. "But stories about the murder aren't going to get this building stopped."

"Maybe not. But right now it's a crime scene, so no work is going to be done for a while."

Frank nodded and gave a grim smile. "Getting murdered is probably the first useful thing Tilson did in his life."

I walked back out to the street and went past the building site. I was tempted to take a look around to see if there was anything the police had missed, but I knew that at least one neighbor would spot me doing it. I figured the potential trouble with the police was more than snooping was worth.

I rang the bell at Kay's house. A short, trim woman wearing jeans and a t-shirt opened the door for me.

"I was hoping you'd stop by here," she said, "I'm Kay Berlison. You're from the newspaper, right?"

"How did you know?"

She blushed slightly. "I called Jennifer right after you left her house."

"You folks really keep an eye on each other," I said.

"I'm sure some folks would just call us nosy, but I like to think it's because we're a small community here, and we watch out for each other. C'mon inside. I just made a fresh pot of coffee. Would you like that, or do you prefer tea?"

I expressed my preference for coffee, and she led me to the back of the house and into a brightly lit kitchen. Although not the most modern, it looked exceptionally well maintained. I settled down at the kitchen table while she poured me a cup of coffee and easily convinced me that I should have a slice of homemade coffee cake. For the first few minutes all I did was enjoy the homemade cake, one of the things I missed since Gran left, but finally I decided that I should start earning my living.

"Frank Taylor told me about his run-in with Merv Tilson. It's lucky you were there and had the foresight to call the police."

"I helped a little bit. But it was really Mr. Manning who saved the day. He interposed himself between Frank and Tilson. And when he knocked Tilson down, a lot of the fight went out of him."

"Did you get any sense that this was a long-standing dispute between the two men?"

"Not really. But I'm afraid Mr. Tilson seemed like the kind of man who created disputes wherever he went. You know the type of man I mean. The sort who always responds with anger when someone disagrees with him in even the smallest particular, and who usually expresses that anger in physical violence."

"Did you see Mr. Tilson around the work site yesterday morning or the night before?"

"No, and that was rather odd, because Tilson was around a lot. Sometimes he'd be there for an hour or two in the morning, just sitting in his truck reading the paper. Other times he'd stroll down to the river. Often he'd be back again in the afternoon, and a few times he even showed up at night. It was like he came at random times, hoping to catch someone trespassing." Kay paused and took a sip of her coffee. "The only people I actually saw there yesterday were you, and Mr. Manning, and that Mr. Donovan."

"You've met Mr. Donovan before."

"Oh, yes. He came around to all our houses before the construction began to introduce himself and say how happy he was to be moving to the neighborhood. I didn't tell him what I really thought about that; it wouldn't have been polite. But I gather Frank gave him an earful."

"But you didn't see Merv Tilson earlier that morning?"

"I hadn't actually seen him since the morning of the day before. He was looking over the site that day."

"And throwing rocks at me," I added, and told Kay the story of my attack.

"That's terrible, but I'm afraid very typical of Tilson. The property lines of our houses do extend down to within three yards of the banks of the river, so I suppose that technically you were trespassing, but that's no reason to attack someone."

"When you said that you hadn't actually *seen* him yesterday, what exactly did you mean?"

"Well, my bedroom is in the back of the house on the side toward the construction, and I usually sleep with my bedroom window open a crack because I like the fresh air. Sometime before dawn I heard what I thought was Tilson's truck."

"How did you know it was his truck?"

"He has a bad muffler, so it makes a bit of a racket. I checked the clock and it was four-forty-five. Then the truck went silent, so I figured someone had turned off the engine. I must have drifted back to sleep because about fifteen minutes later I heard the muffler again and listened to the truck pull away."

"Have you told anyone about this?" I asked.

She shook her head. "I meant to tell the police, but the state police officer who came to question me was so abrupt that I forgot all about it. Do you think I should call them right now?"

I shook my head. "I'll let them know."

"Would you like another piece of cake?" Kay offered.

I struggled with my conscience and said no. As we walked to the door, Kay turned to me and said, "You asked me earlier whether Mr. Manning had any grievance with Mr. Tilson. I don't think you could say that, but I got the impression on the day of their little fight that Mr. Manning really didn't like him much. However, I doubt that he disliked him enough to kill him."

"That would take a lot of dislike."

She nodded. "But Tilson *was* a very annoying man."

As I drove back to the office I mentally reviewed what I had learned. Tilson was obnoxious, that I already knew. He'd had a brief fight with Manning. Since I didn't think Manning had a particularly cool head, I wasn't surprised, although it was to Manning's credit that he was defending Frank. The most valuable piece of information was Kay's report of hearing Tilson's truck at the site before dawn. Did Tilson meet someone there at four-forty-five in the morning and get into a fight that ended in his death? Or was he already dead, and the murderer used his truck to transport the body to the work site? But why dump Tilson somewhere he was bound to be discovered? Okay, my stroll in the woods probably made it sooner than otherwise, but I doubted that a work crew could be there very long without spotting him. Why not toss his body in a ravine or bury him in a forest?

I decided that once I got back to the office, I'd have to get my emotions under control and call Farantello. He knew everything I knew and maybe more. The more was what I wanted to find out.

CHAPTER 12

Dear Auntie Mabel,

My boyfriend is like super clean. He takes two showers a day, carries sanitary hand wipes, and washes his clothes after wearing them once. The thing that really bothers me is that he always carries a toothbrush and toothpaste around with him, so whenever we eat out, he can go in the men's room and brush his teeth after a meal. I think that's too weird, but he says it will keep his teeth from rotting. Who's right?

Weirded Out

Dear Weirded Out,

Maybe you are both right. Your boyfriend does seem to have an obsessive concern with cleanliness, but let's face it, there are worse things in a guy. Most of them would rather wear the same clothes for a week, shower only when it rains, and brush their teeth when the moon is full. Maybe your boyfriend is a little weird, but it's a lot more fun kissing a guy with minty-fresh breath.

Auntie Mabel

When I got back to the *Chronicle,* the first thing I did was retrieve my lunch bag from the communal refrigerator. I hauled out my tuna on rye and gobbled it up while I opened my mail for the day, or, to be more precise, Auntie Mabel's mail. I always divide the mail into three piles: the ones that just complain and don't ask questions—these I throw away; the ones that are too obscene to print even in a censored form—these I throw away; the final pile are the ones that I answer. Usually fifty percent of the letters that come in end up in the answerable pile.

As I sorted through the letters, I was thinking to myself what a shame it was that Donovan was going to be able to build his monstrosity of a house in that nice little neighborhood. Maybe the residents couldn't really expect that land to remain empty, but they didn't deserve to have a mini-Versailles put up on the lot. I wondered if there was anything I could do, not as a representative of the newspaper of course, but as a private citizen.

Russ Jones walked across the newsroom. It was unusual to see him this late in the day. He always attended committee meetings in the evening and either wrote his stories late at night or came in early in the morning. Since the *Chronicle* is an afternoon paper, it pretty much has to be ready to go to press by mid-morning.

"Can I ask you a question, Russ?" I called out.

He swiveled gracefully in mid-stride and came over to my desk.

"At your service," he said with an arched eyebrow.

Russ was a mild flirt, but it never amounted to anything. He was so good looking and fundamentally ambitious that I didn't think he was going to go slumming by getting involved with anyone at the *Chronicle*.

"What is the normal governmental procedure for getting permission to build a new house?"

"Well, you or your contractor has to go to the building commissioner's office and fill out an application for a permit. The commissioner's office checks out your deed to the property and also looks over your plans and decides whether they meet the requirements with regard to setbacks and the sitings on the lot. They also look into any environmental restrictions involving the land. When all that is done to their satisfaction, you'll be issued a permit to build that has to be posted in a clearly visible place on the property."

"Sounds like a long process."

"It's not very long if you're only looking to build one home in a residential neighborhood. But if you were planning to put up a development or a commercial building, it can take quite a while, and it usually ends up going before the city council."

"Does the building commissioner really look into the environmental effects of putting up a building?"

"He sends someone to take a look around. If there is a wetland or some other area that might be a home to God's protected creatures, he'll give it a closer look. But otherwise, the inspection is pretty perfunctory."

"Is there any way for a particular piece of land to get a more extensive examination?"

Russ paused. "Are we talking about that piece of property where you recently found a dead man?"

I blushed at being found out. "Actually I am. It seems a shame that the guy who owns the property is going to ruin the neighborhood by putting up a garish house."

"I take it that having dead bodies on the lot won't discourage him?"

"Not likely. Knowing the owner, he probably thinks it'll give the property character. What about the Historical Commission? The house will block public access to the Vandersnooten Memorial."

"Well, the best course of action is to have one of the neighbors who abuts the property file a request for an extended evaluation of the site on whatever grounds you can think of. Probably it's best to get a lawyer to handle that because it can quickly become litigious."

"Can you recommend a lawyer?"

Russ frowned. "Let me think about it. Maybe I can come up with someone who wouldn't charge an arm and a leg. I'll get back to you."

Giving me a friendly nod, he loped off across the room and out the door.

Again I considered giving Farantello a call and then thought better of it. The one time in the past when I'd been involved in a murder, he had severely limited what I could put into my newspaper story about the crime. I knew the state police would already be involved, and the last thing Farantello would want was to have important information become public knowledge. I was sympathetic to his point of view, but I didn't want my story limited to a warmed-over version of what I'd written yesterday. I decided that in tomorrow's piece I would mention the controversy over building on the site and mention the confrontation Merv Tilson had had with the neighbors, but I would not report the shoving match with Manning, or Kay Berlison's truck in the night. In the rest of the story I would fill in the background of who owned the land and who the contractor was on the site. Tomorrow morning, after my story was handed in, I would call Michael and give him the information it contained in return for whatever he could tell me. He might not be happy, but he'd play ball.

I spent the rest of the afternoon wearing my Auntie Mabel cap and left a few minutes early to get ready for Ronnie's dinner.

Johnson's Farmhouse Restaurant is a humble name for one of the two rather elegant restaurants in Ravensford. It has a park-like setting, spacious rooms, and a very nice American menu. It was often the place chosen by local people to celebrate a special occasion, which was exactly what worried me. I had a bad feeling about the special occasion Ronnie and Everett were celebrating.

Ronnie, Everett, and Krank were already seated when I arrived, and I took my place with Krank on my left. I'd just settled down when Manning walked in.

"Hey, Nick, glad you finally got here," Everett said with a broad smile.

Nick nodded to Everett, not exactly sharing the happiness of the moment. When he looked at me, he stopped to stare. I knew I had cleaned up pretty well, but I was surprised by the intensity of his gaze.

"You look particularly lovely tonight," he said as he sat down on my right.

I checked for a note of sarcasm, but couldn't find one.

"Thank you," I replied.

"She most certainly is lovely," an assertive little voice barked from my left.

"Krank!" Nick exclaimed with an expression of disgust. "What in God's name are you doing here? Are you still trying to sell your art to Everett?"

Sebastian leaned across me and said, "I am here as Ms. Magee's escort."

Nick leaned across me from the other side. "Oh you are, are you?" he said, appearing ready to grab the man by the scruff of the neck and carry him outside.

With two men leaning across me from each side working themselves up to a fight, I had a bad feeling that if I didn't intervene, I was going to serve as the battleground.

"Sebastian is my escort for tonight," I said to Nick in a cool voice.

"He is?" Nick asked, surprised.

"Well, you never asked me to come with you. And since Sebastian and I have already established a relationship, I thought it would be most appropriate for him to accompany me."

"You and Krank have a relationship?" asked Nick, sinking

97

back in his chair as if he were feeling faint.

"A business relationship, of course," I added after a minute spent enjoying the stunned expression on Nick's face.

"Laura's newspaper is going to do an article on my exhibit at the college, and the general manager of the newspaper is helping me get into a major New York gallery," Sebastian explained.

Nick looked at me as if hoping I would break into uproarious laughter, thus confirming this was all a particularly unfunny joke.

"Sebastian is really very skilled," I said. "An up and coming young sculptor."

"I plan to buy one of his pieces to add to my collection," Everett announced happily.

Nick stared at his friend as if he had never before seen this traitorous side of him. "To add to what collection? Your collection of classic beer bottles?"

Everett's face took on a bewildered expression.

"He has to start somewhere," Ronnie said, jumping to her boyfriend's defense. "I happen to think Everett has a very discerning artistic eye."

Ronnie looked around the table with an expression that challenged anyone to disagree with her. Everyone appeared too stunned to offer a refutation, except for Everett, who had lost the thread of the conversation and was smiling vaguely.

Finally, I decided it was time for me to support my friend.

"Investing in the work of a new artist is always something of a gamble, but just consider those people who paid a few thousand in the early twentieth century for a Picasso. The financial returns can be substantial."

"And the purchaser would have the additional pleasure of living with one of my sculptures," said Sebastian, giving Nick a huge smile.

Nick stared at him, silently saying he'd rather live with a

cobra. His eyes traveled around the table as if he'd suddenly found himself sitting with a gathering of serial killers rather than friends.

A waiter appeared and opened a bottle of champagne with a loud pop. Ronnie clapped her hands excitedly, drawing male attention to her ample chest, which was not very well concealed behind the open lacework bodice of her dress. She was almost bouncing up and down in her chair as the waiter poured champagne in our fluted glasses.

Finally, she said, "Listen up, everyone. We are not actually here to celebrate Sebastian's good fortune, although that is really great. Everett and I invited you all here because we'd like to make an announcement."

Everett looked at Ronnie, and this time his expression was focused and showed more determination than I had come to expect from him in our short acquaintance.

"Ronnie and I would like to announce our engagement," he declared.

I glanced over at Nick and saw dismay in his eyes that I knew matched my own. This was far too fast, especially for two people not exactly known as thinkers.

"Congratulations!" Krank shouted instantly and raised his glass in a toast.

Nick and I slowly followed suit.

"Do you have a ring to show us?" Sebastian asked Ronnie, apparently as excited by the whole thing as the happy couple.

Everett blushed. I hadn't seen many grown men blush before, and it struck me once again how much of a boy-man this tall, blond, handsome multimillionaire actually was. I only hoped that Ronnie was willing to tackle the commitment necessary to make marriage to such an immature man work.

"Ronnie said she didn't want a ring," Everett stammered. "She wanted to make it clear to everyone that she isn't marrying me for my money."

"Would she go as far as to sign a pre-nuptial agreement to that effect?" Nick asked in a hard voice.

"Of course I would," Ronnie said without hesitation.

I looked across at my friend, surprised at the unusual note of confidence in her tone. There was something subtly different about her. She still had the baby doll figure and the wanton curls that seemed to promise nothing but mindless pleasure to a man, but there was a new firmness around her mouth that suggested a recent transformation into greater maturity.

"I don't think that would be an appropriate foundation for a marriage," Everett said, giving Nick a warning glance. "Marriage has to be based on trust." He stopped speaking, and his usual bewildered expression returned, as if he couldn't quite recall what his next thought had been.

"Lots of wealthy men have their brides-to-be sign pre-nups," said Nick.

"I'm not lots of wealthy men," Everett shot back.

Nick raised an eyebrow in apparent surprise at his friend's defiance, but remained silent.

"Why all this talk of money and business?" Sebastian broke in. "This is a time to celebrate the happiness of the couple-to-be."

Saying that, he leaned over and gave Ronnie a resounding kiss on the lips. For a moment I thought that Everett was going to knock the little man across the room, but then Ronnie laughed. She jumped up from her chair and, giggling girlishly, came over and gave me a hug. Even Nick managed to rouse himself enough to give her a quick peck on the cheek. By the time she had returned to her seat, Sebastian had launched into a long and entertaining story about attending the engagement party of the Countess Hollenzollen.

When Sebastian finished, Ronnie whispered something in

Everett's ear.

"We have one other announcement to make," Everett said.

"God, she can't be pregnant already," Nick muttered so low, only I could hear. I shot him a warning glance.

"I am going to sell the family cottage in the hills."

Nick, who had just taken a drink of water, began to choke. I gave him a resounding slap on the back.

"Are you trying to fracture my spine?" he asked, suddenly cured.

I smiled politely. "Only trying to help."

"Why are you selling the house?" Nick shouted across to Everett, not able to keep the indignation out of his tone.

"It's old," Everett replied. Everyone remained silent, waiting for him to say more, but when he went back to his meal as if that was all that needed to be said. Ronnie hurriedly picked up the thread.

"It's a big old place. It doesn't have central air conditioning, and it would cost a fortune to heat in winter if we decided to spend any time there. The view is terrific, of course, but the grounds are just too large to maintain without an army of gardeners."

"But I thought you liked it out here?" Nick asked his friend.

Everett glanced up from his plate and spoke through his half-full mouth. "I do."

"Everett plans to replace it. He wants to build a new house on a different location in the Berkshires," Ronnie explained.

"The old place reminds me too much of my grandma," Everett said.

I figured this was another story of a lonely rich boy kept apart from other children his age, playing only with adults who were paid to be his friend.

"We realize that we've known each other for only a couple of days, so we plan to have our engagement last until the new house is complete. Then we'll be married there. And of course we'd like you to be the architect," Ronnie said to Nick.

"Will you do that?" Everett asked his friend with an anxious smile, as if his request bordered on the unreasonable.

"I'd be happy to," Nick replied.

I smiled to myself at how smartly Nick had been outmaneuvered. How could he object to Everett's relationship with Ronnie if he was going to be closely involved in designing their future home? I wondered if this had been entirely Ronnie's idea. If so, I was sure that Everett had needed no convincing to give his best friend the job.

After that, as if by unspoken agreement, everyone kept the conversation focused on superficial issues until the meal was over. It wasn't until Nick and I were standing alone together in front of the restaurant waiting for the valet to get our cars that the marriage question reemerged.

"What are we going to do about this?" Nick asked, the pain obvious on his face.

"I'm not sure there's anything that we can do."

Nick shook his head. "There has to be. Even you have to admit that this is awfully fast. Ronnie has decided to get Everett to marry her, and he's so besotted that he'll do anything she says. He'd jump off a cliff if she suggested it."

"I don't think your friend is quite the passive lump of clay you imagine. Maybe he feels that he's finally found somebody who will be patient enough to help him grow up. And anyway, it will probably take a long time to build the new house. That will give them an opportunity to get to know each other."

"In the meantime, all Ronnie's going to do is help him spend his money."

"If that's what you think, then you should definitely refuse the commission to build their house."

I turned away as the valet brought my car.

"Wait a minute," Nick said, touching my arm. "I'm just trying to protect Everett."

"Did it ever occur to you that maybe he doesn't need your protection? And, in fact, maybe you have as much growing up to do as Everett."

I stuffed a dollar in the valet's hand and got into my car. Without looking back at Nick, I pulled down the driveway.

Chapter 13

Dear Auntie Mabel,

I recently adopted a stray cat named Blinky. Blinky is very sweet, and I find having a pet relieves much of the stress and anxiety that builds up in me during the course of my workday. My husband, however, claims that he has an allergy to cats, and that being around Blinky is making him ill. I have never heard about his allergy to cats before, and my husband refuses to be tested by a doctor who might be able to treat his supposed allergy. He keeps saying that either Blinky goes or he will.

Animal Lover

Dear Animal Lover,

Many people do have a genuine allergic reaction to cat dander. Your husband may be one of those people. An allergist could give him shots to lessen the effects of being around Blinky. Since your husband refuses to see a doctor, it sounds to me like he's making this a test of your love. Try to reason with him one more time and, if that doesn't work, turn the tables on him and call his bluff. Tell him that if he wants to stay, he has to accept Blinky. I have a feeling he may suddenly be cured. If not, you'll have to decide which of them you want to have around.

Auntie Mabel

I came in to work very early the next morning, and managed to have my story on Sam's desk by seven-thirty. He didn't smile or say anything, but I think I received a slight nod, which I took as a favorable sign. I spent the rest of the morning answering Auntie Mabel letters and giving Mrs. Pear some advice with the classifieds.

By early afternoon my mind was wandering as I watched the motes of dust floating around in the rays of sun coming in the large southeast window. Since the paper would be on the stands by now, it was too late for Farantello to ask me to leave anything out. I figured I could safely call him.

That was when the phone rang. It was Farantello.

"I read your story in today's paper."

"So soon."

"I have a deputy assigned to bring it to me as soon as it arrives."

"Don't tell me. You thought I gave too much away."

"I didn't think it was so bad, but the state police detective in charge of the case isn't very happy. Of course, he'd like the public to forget there was a murder until he's got it solved. So expect a visit from a Lieutenant Jeffrey Laurence sometime in the near future."

"That sounds swell. If you run into him before he comes calling on me, you might tell him he should thank me for keeping the best piece of information out of the paper."

"What's that?"

"I'll tell you if you agree to answer my questions."

"Depends on the questions."

I figured that was fair, and went on to tell him what Kay had said about hearing a truck in the early hours of the morning.

"Why didn't she mention it to the state cop who went around there interviewing everyone?"

"She said the guy who talked to her was intimidating. She got flustered and forgot."

Farantello sighed. "I wish those state guys would remember

that sometimes the local officers can get more information than they can. We know how to talk to our own people."

"Maybe they need more human relations training."

Farantello was silent for a moment, which I knew couldn't be a good sign.

"How well do you know Nick Manning?"

"I met him for the first time two days ago, and he was at Ronnie and Everett's engagement dinner last night."

"Ronnie's engaged?"

"That's right. Feel free to express your surprise."

Farantello knew Ronnie pretty well. He and I were still together during the first couple of months Ronnie lived with me, so he saw quite a lot of her.

"I am surprised. It makes me want to meet her fiancé."

"Trust me, even if you met him, it would still be a mystery as to why Ronnie picked him."

"Does he have a lot of money?"

"Now you sound like Manning. He's trying to protect his friend from Ronnie the gold digger."

"So Ronnie's fiancé is a friend of Manning's?"

I gave Farantello a brief summary of the intertwined relationships.

"Thanks for the background. It may be helpful when we go to interview Manning this afternoon."

"Why? Is he a suspect?"

"Well, there is that other little item you left out of your story about Manning decking Tilson."

"Yeah, but that only happened because Tilson attacked Frank Taylor."

"Taylor is on our list as well."

"You can't think that Taylor murdered Tilson just because of a minor altercation."

"Maybe Tilson came around later and wanted to settle things

with Taylor. That could be why Berlison heard his truck early in the morning. Tilson could have underestimated how tough the old guy was."

"Right. An overweight seventy-year-old can take a muscular and violent forty-year-old any day of the week."

"There's always the element of surprise, or maybe Taylor and Manning got together and decided to get rid of Tilson."

"What would be their motive? Taylor doesn't want the Donovan house built, and Manning is the architect. They aren't on the same side."

"I guess we'll know more about that after we've interviewed them both."

"Are you really serious about this?"

"I'm not particularly," Farantello said, "but Lieutenant Laurence is."

"And he's in charge?"

"You've got it."

"Then good luck, because you're going to need it."

"Yeah."

"Well, I have a couple of questions for you. Where did Donovan stay last night? I met him at Everett's place in the Berkshires, and I doubt that he drove all the way back to Boston from there, then out here again the next morning."

"You're right. He stayed at the Sheraton in Springfield."

"So he didn't spend the night in Ravensford?"

"I guess he isn't in to bed and breakfasts or second-rate motels."

"He could have stayed at the Collins Inn; that's pretty nice."

"Probably he likes the amenities of a larger hotel."

I was silent for a moment.

"What are you thinking?" Farantello asked.

"He could still have driven out here from Springfield in half an hour and met Tilson at the building site and killed him."

"Why would he meet him at four-thirty in the morning? And for that matter, why would Donovan kill him?"

"I'm not sure yet," I admitted. "I'm just saying it's possible."

I could almost hear Farantello's shrug.

"Another thing, where did Tilson stay in Ravensford?"

"The Drake Falls Motel."

"And how long had he been in town?"

"Two and a half weeks, according to the desk clerk at the Drake Falls. That's how long they've been working on the house."

"Okay."

"Why did you want to know?"

"I was just thinking that possibly Tilson's death had nothing to do with Donovan or the house he's building. Tilson sounds like the kind of guy who could easily have made a few enemies during his time in town. Maybe you guys should check around and see if he's made any recent enemies."

"People who would kill him and dump his body at the building site?"

"If they wanted to direct suspicion away from themselves."

Farantello was silent for a moment. "I'll suggest the idea to Laurence, but he's in charge."

"Yeah, you already said that."

I hung up the phone, spun my chair around to face the room, and almost jumped. Standing right in front of me was a short thin woman. She couldn't have weighed more than ninety pounds soaking wet, and her lank, mousey-brown hair hung down to her shoulders, as if she had just come out of the shower. I even glanced out the window to see if some rain had sprung up to account for the woman's woebegone appearance, but the sun was still shining without a hint of a cloud in the sky. I decided the woman must have her own personal storm following her around.

"I'm Bibi Grouse."

I stared at her, waiting for more. The woman, who couldn't have been more than twenty-five, sighed heavily, as if she'd already been through a long lifetime of going unrecognized.

"The woman out at the desk . . . Mrs. Peach?"

"Pear," I corrected.

"Whatever. She told me to come back here."

"Okay," I said, still puzzled.

"Russ mentioned that you needed a lawyer."

"That's right," I said, giving her what I guess she interpreted as a skeptical glance.

"I'm a lawyer. I'm getting ready to set up my own practice in town. I'm Dorothy Farnsworth's granddaughter."

"Dorothy Farnsworth who owns the antique store?"

Bibi nodded. "I'm helping her out in the shop until I can get established. She was real excited about this because it involves something historical, and Russ said that helping you would be good experience. People always say that when they want you to work for free."

I hadn't thought about payment. I wasn't sure how much the neighborhood retirees were going to be willing to cough up or whether I'd have to try to cover the bill.

"I can guarantee that if you find a way to block the construction of the Donovan house, someone will find a way to reward you." Even if it is only in baked goods from Kay, I thought.

"Well, nobody has to get their checkbook out just yet. From what I've learned so far, the Historical Commission only has the authority to recommend that specific houses not be torn down or renovated in 'ways that would diminish their historical significance.' Since there is no house currently on the site where Donovan wants to build, there's nothing the Historical Commission can do."

"Not even to guarantee access to a historical marker?"

109

"Russ mentioned that to me. From what the woman at the Historical Commission said, there is an alternate route to the marker, so there's nothing for us there."

"Then we're doomed."

Bibi Grouse smiled for the first time, as if she enjoyed being the bearer of bad news.

"Maybe from the historical angle, but there might be some environmental concerns. You and Russ talked about that, didn't you?"

"Right. How can we find out?"

"One of the abutters would have to apply for an extended review."

"Do you think we'd find anything that would stop construction?"

Bibi shrugged. "I have a friend who works for the state EPA, and she says that building at the top of a slope overlooking a body of water is always tricky because of the danger of creating a run-off situation."

"You mean a stretch of the river might silt up as a result of Donovan's building on the slope."

"Nothing quite so dramatic. But there's no way of telling whether there are any chemicals in the soil that might be harmful to creatures in the river. According to my friend, if you knew what was lurking in the dirt under your feet, you'd never let them touch the ground." Grouse smiled thinly. "These EPA guys get a little carried away sometimes."

"So you think we've got something here, I mean legally?"

Bibi's smile disappeared, replaced by her normal frown. "Who knows with the law?"

I was tempted to suggest that she should know since she was a lawyer.

"The law is what the courts say it is," the woman recited as if it were the only thing she remembered from her last semester's class.

"I see. Can you come up with anything more productive than that?" I asked, resisting the urge to reach across the desk and shake some enthusiasm into her.

"Harassment," she announced.

"Harassment?"

She nodded. "Like I said, we request an extended inspection. That means the property will be crawling with folks taking soil and water samples. We might even get a couple of biologists poking around under rocks and bushes trying to find an endangered species or two."

"Do you think they'll find anything?"

Bibi shrugged her sloping shoulders. "Who knows? People tell me that you'd be surprised what you can find in a tiny ecosystem. All you need is some lizard with a lot of friends in politics. And like I said, the point is harassment. All this will at least delay construction for a few days, and if we should find something, Donovan might decide to bail out rather than enter into a long, contentious proceeding."

"He doesn't strike me as a quitter."

"Most people don't like bad publicity. So just say the word, and we'll find out."

I turned away from her to gaze out the window. I was torn between the possibility of stopping Donovan in his tracks, and a wave of guilt at making Nick's life more difficult. Although why I should have any reluctance on that score after he had virtually called Ronnie a gold digger was beyond me.

"I'll let you know," I said, turning back to the woman.

Bibi shrugged as if accustomed to being put off and handed me a business card.

"Antic Antiques," I read.

"Yeah, my grandmother's shop. My cell number is on the

back, but you can leave a message for me at the shop during the day."

Just as I stood up to escort Bibi out, Sebastian came walking across the office.

"I have a bear with me," he announced.

Bibi's eyes grew wide, and she peered behind Sebastian as if hoping to catch a glimpse of the bruin.

"Ah, and who is this lovely creature?" Sebastian shouted with delight, seizing Bibi's hand and pressing it to his lips.

I performed the introductions, all the time aware that Bibi's shoulders had gone from what had appeared to be a permanent hunch into a pressed-back posture that made even her emaciated figure close to voluptuous. At the same time, her expression of world-weary irony was replaced with a doe-eyed simper of adoration. Although they were the same height, she managed to look up at Sebastian as if he were a giant among men.

"Do you want to see my bear?" he asked Bibi.

"Oh, yes," the woman gushed as if this was an offer she had waited a lifetime to hear.

He nodded happily and disappeared behind Mrs. Pear's counter. A second later he came through, pushing a wheelbarrow containing a canvas sack. Bibi stared at the package oddly, as if wondering why a bear in a bag would struggle so little.

"Put it over here," I said, clearing a space near my desk as Sebastian pushed his slender frame to the limit maneuvering his cargo across the room.

"I will need some help," Sebastian said.

I hurried forward to lend a hand. Bibi followed suit, and we lifted the sack onto the table.

"Is it drugged?" Bibi whispered to me.

I shook my head. Sebastian waited for us to arrange ourselves in the proper position for appreciative viewing. After making sure the sack was untied, he slid the covering off and stood back.

It was beautiful. It was exactly the same design as the bear I had already seen sculpted in wood, but this one was over a foot tall at the shoulder and three feet long from nose to tail, done in white marble.

"It's a statue," Bibi said, the faintest hint of disappointment evident in her voice. "But what a statue!" she exclaimed, recovering quickly.

"Let me show you," Sebastian said. He took Bibi's hand. "Now close your eyes."

She obediently followed his command, placing her hand in his and pressing her eyes firmly shut. Sebastian eased her forward and placed her hand on the bear's pointed muzzle. Slowly he moved her fingers up and down its nose and jaw.

"Feel how proud and erect it is," Sebastian intoned, keeping her fingers moving in continual contact with the stone.

"Yes," Bibi murmured. "Oh, yes."

He slid her hand along the spine of the piece to the rear. He directed her hand along the rump of the bear with long bold strokes.

"Do you feel the power in those muscular haunches?"

"Hmm."

"Imagine those muscles hardening with tension as the bear begins to charge. Can you feel that?"

"Mmm."

I could see that Bibi's pallid complexion was getting a bit rosier and her eyelids were fluttering. Even I had to admit it seemed to be getting a bit warm in the room.

Sebastian gently placed Bibi's hand on the underside of the bear, running her fingers from front to back.

"Here we have his private side, the vulnerable underbelly the bear will reveal only to someone he trusts. Feel his ribs, then move your hand back and feel . . ."

"Oh! Y-e-s!"

By now Bibi was clutching Sebastian as if she would fall over without support.

"It's a very nice piece," I said in a flat voice, resisting the urge to suggest that they go rent a room for the three of them.

Bibi's eyes opened. She looked around herself in surprise as if she'd been away on a long journey.

"I've never seen sculpture that way before," she said, dazed.

Sebastian smiled. "Sculpture is the most sensuous of the arts. I have many more pieces back in my studio. If you have the time, we could go look at some of them now."

"I have lots of time."

Sebastian turned toward me. "Would Mr. Rumson be available to look at this sculpture? I'd like him to have a better idea of my work if he is going to attempt to get me into a New York gallery."

"He isn't here right now."

"Hmm. Perhaps I could leave the statue here, and you could show it to him when he comes in."

"I'm not sure how good our security is," I said. "People come in and out of here all day long."

"Perhaps you could put it in Mr. Rumson's office. Does the door lock?"

I nodded. I didn't bother to tell him that the key was usually kept on the casement right above the door for easy access when the boss was out. Using the wheelbarrow, we transported the bear down the hall. I quickly grabbed the key from over the door when Sebastian wasn't looking and let us in to Wally's office. Once we had found a temporary home for Bruno in a corner of the office, we returned to the reception area. After shaking Sebastian's hand several times and bidding goodbye to Bibi, I watched them leave the office together.

"That guy in black is a fast worker," Prudence Pear said. "Sometimes those skinny guys have more juice than you'd give them credit for at first glance."

"I suppose. Small guy, small girl, a natural couple."

"Mr. Pear wasn't a big man, but he had a lot more energy than you'd think on first meeting him."

"I'm sure he did," I said, turning to go back to my office. The last thing I wanted to hear about were the exploits of the virile, if now dead, Mr. Pear.

"You weren't interested in that skinny guy for yourself, were you?" Mrs. Pear asked, delaying my departure.

"No." The word came out a bit louder than I had intended, making the denial sound forced.

"I just wondered because of the expression on your face. Like maybe you envied that stick of a girl a little bit."

"Maybe I do, a bit," I admitted. "What single person doesn't feel a twinge of envy whenever a couple goes by?"

"You can do better than him."

"He's a gifted artist."

"So what? You need a robust, good-looking guy. Not some scrawny artist. But you're never going to find one, not with the way you've been acting."

"What do you mean?"

"You think I don't see things? Two months ago it was that hunk from the furniture company here to sign the contract for new desks. He was drooling all over you, and there you were acting like he was no better than a piece of furniture himself."

"I don't see . . ."

"Then there was the guy who came around with the promotional tickets to the playhouse. A little older, maybe, and more distinguished, but a matinee idol if I ever saw one. He couldn't take his eyes off you. Didn't he even offer you front-row seats if you'd meet him after the show for a drink?"

"Well, I guess . . ."

"And you gave him some line about being busy that night. Said it in a voice that would have frozen a lava flow, as I recall. And just two weeks ago, there was that really cute fellow from the chamber of commerce . . ."

"I don't date handsome men. That's my new rule," I interrupted.

Mrs. Pear stared at me with as much amazement as if I had just announced that I always walked on my hands or only bathed in molasses.

"Well, that's a damned stupid rule," she sputtered. "That's like saying you never eat food that tastes good."

"Handsome men are superficial and chronically unfaithful."

Mrs. Pear leaned across the desk and pushed her face right up to mine until I could smell the tobacco on her breath.

"I thought you were pretty smart, Laura. Didn't your mother ever teach you not to judge a book by its cover? An ugly man can be just as unfaithful as a handsome one."

"But he has fewer opportunities," I snapped back.

Mrs. Pear paused. "I'll grant you that. Lord knows, Mr. Pear, in his prime, turned many a woman's head. But I never worried because I knew I was the one he loved. Sure, it kept me on my toes, knowing there was all sorts of competition out there. I worked to hang on to my girlish figure and kept my dye job up to date. Still, I always had confidence in Mr. Pear because he had lots to choose from, and I was the one he picked. At least he didn't marry me because no one else would have him."

I looked at the wiry little woman. Her face was covered with wrinkles, and she had probably never been what anyone would call beautiful. I'd never seen a picture of Mr. Pear, so I didn't know if he had actually been as Mrs. Pear described him. One thing was for certain, however. Mrs. Pear had thought he was handsome, and being loved by a man she thought was handsome had been tremendously important in her life.

"I'll think about what you've just said," I promised.

"See that you do," Mrs. Pear replied, slipping a pack of cigarettes out of her desk drawer and heading outside.

I settled down once again behind my desk. I had lied to Mrs. Pear. There was no way I was going to reconsider my rule. The last three men in my life had been what I would call good looking. Even though Farantello was less than traditionally handsome, he was still a hunk in a soulful way. And all three had brushed me aside for new girlfriends or ex-wives. Frankly, I was tired of being replaced. I also suspected that there was something superficial about loving a man for his looks. You should love a man for his inner being. So now I was on the hunt for an average-looking guy with a scintillating personality. I knew there had to be thousands of them out there.

For some reason I just hadn't found one.

Chapter 14

Dear Auntie Mabel,

My girlfriend Mona is a wonderful person. I have been seeing her for two years, and we usually have a great time together. But recently she seems to get upset easily and becomes verbally abusive. I don't know how to behave around Mona anymore. Should I just put up with her change in behavior and hope it's temporary?

Bewildered

Dear Bewildered,

If Mona realizes that her behavior is out of control, she may be willing to get help. A complete physical followed by anger management counseling might help. If Mona is unwilling to seek treatment, then it's time to find a more mellow girlfriend.

Auntie Mabel

I decided I should get out of the office before Mrs. Pear was through with her cigarette and wanted to give me more unsolicited romantic advice. So it seemed like a good time to check out the Drake Falls Motel where Merv Tilson had stayed. The motel got its name because it was about two miles north of the center of town near a spot where one of the tributaries of the Ravensford River comes down out of the hills, forming a waterfall. Not much by Niagara standards, it was a drop of about twenty feet, enough that the town had built a small park there that's a popular place for newlyweds to be photographed once they've driven away the ever-present ducks that come around wanting to be fed.

As I swung on to Oak Street and headed out of town, I realized that the sun streaming in my car windows was no longer the shivery white of winter, but the robust, warm rays of spring. Although April can be a back-and-forth month in New England, today was clearly a day that fell on the spring side. A few minutes spent in silent celebration of the end of winter and the Drake Falls Motel came up on my left. I pulled into a gravel driveway soft with mud around the edges, one of the hazards that came with the end of winter, and parked in front of the office.

The motel had to be at least fifty years old. It was designed in the old style of New England motels; the building was one long strip divided up into identical units. In the summer a single chair would have stood next to each door for those who found the passing traffic more interesting than sitting in their room or watching the small television chained to the wall right across from the bed. Parking was directly in front of the door, convenient for the transport of luggage, although a bit noisy when guests chose to leave before dawn.

I walked in the office and my nose was immediately overwhelmed by the scent of mustiness and pine. The walls and counter were constructed of knotty pine. Not the cheap kind that passes for wood paneling today, but the thick, real pine common to the fifties. I was amazed that it still gave off a pungent aroma, probably one the chubby-faced woman of late middle age behind the desk scarcely noticed anymore.

I introduced myself, telling her I was a reporter looking into the recent death in town of one of her customers. The woman, who said her name was Sarah Langston, nodded her head.

"He was one of our long-term residents. He stayed almost

three weeks. We don't get many people who hang around here more than two nights, and one is the usual."

"Not that much to see in Ravensford?"

She nodded. "Plus, there are nicer motels in Springfield and farther east toward Boston. And we're a few miles off the Pike, so a traveler has to take the trouble to find us."

"I'll bet your rates are good."

"This time of the year, they're great—under forty dollars a night."

"Do you think that's why Tilson stayed here?"

She smiled, making her cheeks dimple. "I'm sure of it. He told me that he got a per diem amount when he was on the road, and if he didn't spend it all, he could pocket the difference. That was probably a tidy amount, although I doubt he had much left over at the end of the day."

"Why do you say that?"

"He drank," she said in the same tone as she might have said that he routinely drowned kittens.

"How do you know?"

"I smelled it on his breath one time when he came around in the late afternoon to pay his bill. And a man who will drink in the afternoon . . ." Her lips tightened judgmentally. ". . . well, that's probably all he does at night. He didn't have enough work to do, if you ask me."

"I thought he was supposed to be keeping an eye on that building site?"

"Oh, he'd stop by there a few times during the day and maybe a couple of times after it got dark, but that's not enough work to keep a healthy man busy."

"So he drank in between?"

"Not all the time. In the morning he'd come back here around ten o'clock and sleep until afternoon. No wonder, since he wouldn't get back most nights until one or two in the morning. I live in back, and I'd hear him roaring in with that truck of his at all hours."

"So afternoons and evenings, he'd spend a lot of his time drinking. Where did he drink?"

"He asked my husband, George, for some suggestions about places. George isn't a drinking man himself, of course, so I doubt he could help him."

"Do you know if he gave him any suggestions?"

"Hang on a second. I'll go check." The woman disappeared into the back room, and I heard her voice asking the question. I couldn't hear his reply.

I breathed in the ambience of the knotty pine office, wondering how these folks managed to make a living. Ravensford was on the wrong side of the Berkshires for the tourist trade, and as Sarah had said, they were too far from the Mass Pike to pick up travelers looking for somewhere to overnight. I wondered if George had another job, and if running this place was more a hobby than a major source of income.

Sarah reappeared and walked up to the counter.

"George says the only place he mentioned to him was the Collins Inn."

"I think of that more as an inn and restaurant than a bar," I said.

"George doesn't go to bars, but we go out to eat sometimes, and that's one of our favorite places. It does have a separate bar area, and I guess it was the only place George knew about."

I thanked Sarah Langston for her time and walked back to my car. It was almost four o'clock, a little early to hang out in a bar, but I could swing by there and still get home in time to make supper for Ronnie and myself. This was my night to cook.

The Collins Inn is on the west side of town, so I drove back down and around the green and out in the direction of Ravensford College. About a mile before the college was the Collins

Inn, named after Captain Ashcroft Collins. To his family, he was a hero, but history records that he was the only officer George Washington is known to have publicly threatened to horsewhip if he ever laid eyes on him. Fortunately for Millicent Collins, the last surviving relative and owner of the inn, few people read history.

The inn's parking lot was close to empty when I got there. I wasn't surprised. It was too early for the dinner crowd, and there wouldn't be many overnight guests this early in the spring. Five cars were huddled around the side entrance leading to the bar, so I parked over there.

I'd never been in the bar before. I knew parts of the building went back to Revolutionary War times, and over the years the updates had been selective. Just inside the door there was a sign saying that the bar was the oldest part of the structure, going back to 1750. The low ceiling and wide wood floorboards, along with a fireplace you could almost walk into standing up, certainly impressed me as authentic. Less authentic were the imitation oil lamps scattered around the room, and enough decorative rifles, drums, and bunting on the walls to equip a regiment. Like Millicent Collins's style in the restaurant, this was just too much of something that wasn't very good to begin with.

I sat down at the bar and asked for a beer. The guy who got it for me was old enough to be my grandfather, but he seemed friendly and even pushed a bowl of peanuts in my direction. He stood washing glasses within speaking distance, and since I couldn't think of an indirect way of raising the topic, I went with the direct approach.

"I work for the *Chronicle,* and I heard the man whose body was recently found dead at that building site on the other side of town used to drink here." I didn't want to say the man was murdered; that might startle him into keeping quiet.

"You mean that guy they found where that house is going up?"

I nodded.

The bartender paused, then nodded. "Could be. There was a guy who came in here over the last few weeks. He said he had something to do with security at a building site."

"That must be him. Was he in here a lot?"

"Yeah. He'd spend half the afternoon, then come back later on at night."

"Did he come in with anybody else?"

"Nah. He'd talk to the guys who were here once in a while, but he always came in alone."

"Did he ever talk to you about having a problem with anyone?"

The bartender smiled. "He was the kind of guy who could get on a person's nerves when he was sober and was even worse after he'd had a few. I imagine he made enemies."

"Anyone in particular?"

"Not here. We don't let things get out of hand. This is a live-and-let-live kind of bar."

I was running out of questions, so I fell back to my most general one.

"Did anything out of the ordinary ever happen when he was in here?"

The bartender stopped wiping the glass in his hand and thought.

"A little over two weeks ago, he was in here at night, sitting about where you are. He suddenly says to me, 'The things you see when you least expect it.' I asked him what he meant, but he just smiled like he'd won the lottery or something."

I glanced around the bar and didn't see anything significant. Then I looked straight ahead. I shifted over one chair and discovered I could look down a short hall and directly into the lobby of the inn. I wondered if Merv had spotted something there that had sparked his interest, like somebody checking into the inn whom he didn't expect to see. Who would Merv know and be surprised to see here? I asked myself. I figured it had to be someone he knew from back in Boston. Maybe his employer, Max Donovan.

I decided that was worth thinking about, so I finished my beer, left a generous tip, and went home.

CHAPTER 15

Dear Auntie Mabel,

I am having relationship problems. I saw a new man at work named Jake that I wanted to get to know better, so I told my friend Sam, and he asked Jake if he'd like to go out on a date with me. Jake said he wasn't interested because I looked too weird. Auntie Mabel, I am a normal-looking woman in her early twenties, and aside from a few tattoos and an occasional piercing, I am the girl next door. Do you think I am fooling myself into thinking I'm normal?

Pierced But Proud

Dear Pierced,

Men react differently to tattoos and piercings. Some men find them attractive, even erotic, while other men respond less favorably. It sounds as though Jake falls into the second category. I doubt there is anything you can do to change Jake's mind if he refuses to have even one date. Possibly, when he gets to know you better at work, he will come around. If he doesn't, consider it his loss.

Auntie Mabel

"It was the weirdest thing," Ronnie said, collapsing onto the sofa across from me.

She had just finished the washing up. We have a deal that whoever cooks gets out of kitchen duty. I had already gotten settled into the wingback chair that had the best light to read by and perused my most recent article in the *Chronicle* about the Tilson murder. This isn't a vanity thing, where I get all excited at seeing my prose in print. In fact, I usually read my own stuff with a particularly critical eye as to what could have been left out or what vital fact was missed. I then moved on to Russ Jones's piece on the city council meeting. For a guy who didn't come out of the print media, he sure could write. All the facts were there, but at the same time he made the event seem entertaining. I had attended enough of those meetings myself to know making them seem exciting took skill bordering on the miraculous.

I looked up slowly, reluctant to stop reading.

"What was weird?"

"This guy who came around at the dealership today."

"What guy?" I asked.

Ronnie spread her arms out over the back of the sofa and slowly stretched. Then she shook her head.

"He showed up at the service desk, but it didn't make any sense."

"Why? Didn't he have a car?" I asked with a smile.

"Yeah. How did you know?"

I looked up from the paper. "You mean he really didn't have a car."

"I don't think so," Ronnie replied. "At least he didn't have one that he wanted to have serviced. He said that he was look-ing around the showroom and just happened to wander back into the service department."

"And he just had to talk to you?"

"That's what he said. Well, actually, he said quite a bit more than that. He told me how lovely I looked and all that."

I bit my lip at the casualness with which Ronnie accepted male compliments, as if they were her due. It wasn't Ronnie's fault. There probably hadn't been a time in her life, from when she had been just "the cutest itty-bitty baby," that men hadn't made a fuss over her. Now she was more surprised than hurt when she came across the rare man who didn't pay any attention to her.

"So what's weird about that? Lots of guys come on to you in a day."

"Yeah. But he really kept it up. He said that he knew it sounded kind of strange, but would I go out with him. He even showed me his driver's license, so I'd know who he was. His name was Steve Randolph."

I shrugged. "Maybe he was just desperate."

"But that's the thing. He was a real hottie. I mean on a scale of one to ten, he was pushing ten and a half."

"Even cuter than Darling Everett?" I asked.

Ronnie paused. An expression of intense mental concentration came over her face, as if she had been asked to solve a mathematical proof.

"Don't ever tell Everett I said this, but I think today's guy might have been just a smidgen cuter."

I frowned. Was Everett already relegated to the role of "has been"? Had I been wrong to assume that this time things were going to be different?"

"So what did you say to this guy?"

Ronnie hiked herself up on the sofa and adopted an imperious expression.

"I told him I appreciated his attention, but that I was an engaged lady."

"Good for you," I said, surprised and relieved. "Did he go away then?"

"Not right away. He continued at it for a while, trying to change my mind, until I threatened to call my supervisor. Then he left. That's when the totally weird thing happened."

"What?"

"Well, I was kind of looking out the window to see where he went, and a few minutes later I saw a car go by with Nick driving. And I could swear that Steve was sitting right next to him."

"Nick Manning?"

Ronnie nodded.

"Could you have been mistaken? Maybe it was just someone who looked like him."

She gave me a scornful glance.

"Okay, okay. It must have been Nick."

Ronnie's gift of recall was very selective. She might not recognize her family on the street; however, she had a memory bank that contained the picture of every man she'd ever met with his name neatly engraved under it. When it came to women, she only remembered what they wore.

"So, what do you think?" Ronnie persisted. "Was that weird or what?"

"Maybe not quite as weird as you think," I said, heading upstairs to use the phone in my bedroom.

"Leaving already?" Ronnie asked.

"I just remembered a call that I have to make."

"I guess I'll stay here for a while and watch television."

Back in my room, I searched the top of my dresser until I found Nick's card with his phone number. Covering the receiver with a gym sock to disguise my voice, I punched in his number.

When he answered I said, "My name is Maggie Thornbush. Is Steve Randolph there by any chance? He said he was doing something for you today, and he hasn't shown up for our date."

"Sorry," Nick said. "I don't know where Steve is. I dropped him back at his place around two o'clock."

"I knew you were low, Manning, but I didn't know you were this low," I said, uncovering the receiver.

"Laura?" The note of anxiety in his voice quickly turned to resignation. "How did you find out?"

"Ronnie saw you acting as the wheelman in your pathetic little scenario. That was a despicable thing to do."

"Hey, wait a minute. I'll admit that it was a little deceptive."

"A little deceptive? Getting some handsome friend to try to lead Ronnie astray just to break up her engagement to Everett. What were you planning to do? Have your friend Steve take her to a restaurant, and then you and Everett were going to walk in on them?"

Nick's silence indicated I had guessed right.

"Well, it didn't work, did it? Little Ronnie turned out to be a lot more faithful to Everett than you ever imagined, didn't she?"

"Yeah, I guess so," Nick admitted grudgingly.

"You know, I'm tempted to give Everett a call and tell him what you tried to do. I don't think that would do much for your friendship, would it?"

"Please don't do that, Laura. Look, maybe what I did was kind of low, but I had to find out if Ronnie was really ready to commit to one man. You've got to admit she has a history of being flighty. I was only trying to protect Everett."

"By having someone seduce his fiancée. May the Lord protect us from our friends. Who is this Steve Randolph? Some kind of professional gigolo?"

"He's an actor friend of mine."

"Oh, so he's not a real gigolo, but he plays one on television."

"Look, Laura, I'm sorry for what I did, but put yourself in my place. What if Ronnie was like Everett and Everett was like Ronnie. Can't you imagine sending around an attractive woman to see if Everett is true blue?"

I was about to snap "of course not," when I stopped to coolly consider Nick's comment. Regretfully, I had to admit in all honesty such a plan just might have occurred to me, and I might, indeed, have implemented it. Not willing to admit it, I changed the topic slightly.

"Are you at least satisfied now that Ronnie is genuinely devoted to Everett?" I asked.

"I suppose."

"You suppose?"

"You've got to admit that all it really proved is that she wasn't attracted to Steve."

"So what are you going to do? Send a parade of handsome men past her counter every day until she weakens and gives in or until you're certain that you've covered all the possible permutations of male attractiveness?"

"All I'm saying is that Ronnie does seem to be infatuated with Everett right now, but she doesn't strike me as the kind of woman who has much experience with serious commitments. Until I have some proof of that, I'm not going to stop keeping a watchful eye."

"You know, Manning, you have a real gift for being stubborn."

"Coming from you, that's quite a compliment, Magee."

"And I'm telling you right now, I am going to do everything I can to prevent you from achieving both of your pig-headed goals."

"Both?"

"Interfering with Everett and Ronnie, and putting up the Max Donovan house."

"Are you still going on about that? I told you I have no control over what Donovan chooses to do."

"Yes, I am 'still going on about that,' as you so charmingly put it. And soon you'll find out exactly what that means."

"C'mon, Laura, can't you be a bit more reasonable about all this?"

"Oh, so now you're saying women can't be reasonable. You probably think that women are too emotional to have positions of influence."

"Don't put words in my mouth. I never said that."

"But you probably thought it. Men always think more than they say."

"Now who's stereotyping? I'm just asking you to see things from my point of view."

"I have. Unfortunately, your point of view is wrong, Manning."

"We shouldn't be fighting. We should be working together."

"On what?"

"On this Merv Tilson thing. Lieutenant Laurence came to see me today, and he seems convinced that either I did it or you did, or we were in it together, because we are the only two people in town with a grudge against the guy."

"I know I didn't kill him, but I can't speak for you. Not after the trick you pulled today."

"Can't we talk about this?"

"I see no point in continuing this conversation. Goodbye!" Before the phone returned to the cradle, I heard a loud disconnect on the other end.

I searched around until I found Bibi Grouse's card, and gave a call to Antic Antiques.

"Hello," a quivery female voice said.

"Is this Dorothy?"

"That's right, dear."

"This is Laura Magee. Is your niece there, by any chance?"

"Oh, yes. Just a minute."

A few seconds later, Bibi was on the phone. "If there is a God, you've got to give me some work before my allergies become terminal. Today I sorted through the stuff in the attic. Tomorrow I'm supposed to shake out old quilts."

"How soon can you get inspectors on the Donovan site?"

"I need the name of a neighbor to file a complaint."

I gave her Frank Taylor's address and phone number.

"The city works fast when construction has already begun. We should see people on the site by the day after tomorrow. I checked yesterday, and the police have released the area as a crime scene, so there's nothing to stop us."

"Good."

After I hung up I lay down on my bed. My head was pounding, but worse than the pain there was the feeling that I had let my emotions get the better of me. Note to self: whenever you start feeling self-righteous, you're probably wrong. I knew I had been a bit unfair to Manning, but he certainly wasn't being fair to Ronnie. Something about two wrongs not equaling a right ran through my mind, but I pushed it away.

CHAPTER 16

Dear Auntie Mabel,

My middle-aged sister-in-law has recently taken to wearing clothes more appropriate to a teenager. She often goes around in extremely tight short skirts and favors tops that reveal more than anyone should see other than her husband. To me it is embarrassing to have a member of my family making such a fool of herself. We have never been very close, but should I say something to her about her apparent lack of fashion sense?

Suitably Shocked

Dear Shocked,

Since you and your sister-in-law have never been close, your advice would probably not be taken well, and it could lead to family problems far greater than those your sister-in-law's lack of taste has created. You might gently ask your brother if there is some reason she has suddenly taken to dressing so much younger. He may have an explanation or, if he has not been fully aware of how it looks, he might speak to his wife. Be aware, however, that middle-aged women and men who suddenly try to appear younger often have troubles that go far deeper than a lack of fashion sense.

Auntie Mabel

When I settled behind my desk the next morning, having come in the back way, I could hear Mrs. Pear at the front desk. Her voice had the clipped tone that indicated that she was on the edge of losing her temper.

"I've already told you that she isn't here," Mrs. Pear said.

"How can you know that if you haven't looked?"

"Ms. Magee never comes in before eight-thirty."

"Could you just check?"

"I have work to do. I can't be leaving my desk every five minutes to see if various people are here."

I looked at my watch. It had just turned eight-thirty. I figured it was safe to show myself without making Mrs. Pear into a liar. I walked around the corner to the main newsroom. A tall heavy-set man in a business suit, who twenty years ago might have played college football, was standing by the desk, his already florid face getting redder by the minute.

"Is there someone to see me, Mrs. Pear?"

She checked her watch. "It's eight-thirty-one," she said to the man with a triumphant look, as if she had just been proved correct about when the universe began.

"Are you Ms. Magee?" the man asked.

"Would you tell me your name again?" Mrs. Pear asked.

He gave a deep sigh. "I'm Lieutenant Jeffrey Laurence of the Massachusetts State Police."

"This police officer would like to see you," Mrs. Pear said.

I wondered for a minute what would happen if I refused to see him. I could visualize Mrs. Pear clinging to the lieutenant's leg as he tried to get past her desk. I decided it was too early in the morning for anything like that.

"Please send him back," I said.

"As you wish," Mrs. Pear replied, and she nodded her permission for him to come through the swinging gate into the newsroom.

I shook the lieutenant's hand, which was twice the size of mine, and directed him to the chair beside my desk.

He sat down and glanced around the room as if memorizing

it for future reference.

"What do you do for the paper?" he asked.

"This and that," I replied. There was no way I was going to tell him I was Auntie Mabel. Roger St. Clair wanted Auntie Mable's writer to remain confidential, and I wasn't inclined to become generally known as "the advice auntie."

"And the Merv Tilson murder is part of this and that?" he asked.

"Sometimes I handle local news stories when all the other reporters are busy."

The only other reporter handling local news was Russ Jones, but there was no reason the lieutenant had to know how really small an operation we were.

"And part of handling this story is questioning witnesses?"

"Sometimes."

He took a notebook out of the breast pocket of his suit coat.

"That would include questioning Frank Taylor, Kay Berlison, and Sarah Langston."

Damn, I hadn't expected him to already be wise to my visit with Sarah at the motel.

I tried a smile. "You have to talk to people in order to write a story."

He didn't smile back. "You're interfering with a police investigation. By publishing these witness statements, you're making it much harder for us to do our job."

"I don't write about everything I'm told. You'll notice that I didn't say anything about Kay Berlison hearing a truck early on the morning the body was discovered."

"A good thing, or you'd be in a lot more trouble."

"By the way, whatever happened to that truck?"

Lieutenant Laurence paused long enough for me to know that the truck had been found.

"If you don't stop your investigation, I'm going to see to it that there are severe consequences."

I could feel my temper rising. "I bet you don't make threats like that to reporters from the *Globe*. You're just a bully who thinks that because this is a small local newspaper in the western part of the state, you can push us around."

"Who's your editor-in-chief?"

"We have an acting editor-in-chief at the moment." I gave him Wally's name and wished I could be a fly on the wall if they ever met. Let the good lieutenant try to threaten someone who had gone hand-to-hand with the ancient Assyrians. "But he isn't in at the moment."

"When will he be here?"

I shrugged. "Hard to tell. You could try checking back around ten."

Laurence sat there for a long moment. I had a sense that he was getting his emotions under control. Clearly he was starting to get the picture that threatening the *Chronicle* was like punching a fluffy pillow; you expended a lot more energy than was justified by the results.

"Look, Ms. Magee, I can order Detective Farantello not to share any more information with you. That means when we do crack this case, the *Chronicle* will be way behind all the local television stations in carrying the story."

"I'm not sure Farantello is yours to order around. And this works both ways. If I find out anything you don't know, I'll keep it to myself."

"And you might end up on charges of obstruction of justice."

"Which will be hard to prove. And you still won't have solved this case."

Another long sigh. "Why don't we cooperate, then? If you don't publish without my approval, I'll give you whatever information I have."

"Deal," I said, knowing he probably wouldn't live up to the

arrangement any more than I would. "What I'd like to know is whether you've found Tilson's truck."

"Yeah. We found it stripped in an industrial section of Springfield. We figure someone left it in Springfield with the door unlocked and the key in the ignition, hoping that's exactly what would happen."

"Can I print that?"

"Okay. But nothing yet about Kay Berlison hearing the truck on the morning of the murder."

I frowned, then agreed.

"If you know I talked to Sarah Langston, you probably know about Tilson drinking at the Collins Inn." I figured I could volunteer a little to find out what he already knew.

The lieutenant nodded. "We were a few steps behind you, but the bartender told us just what he told you. Do you have any idea what Tilson might have seen?"

"Nope."

He stared at me for a moment as if he suspected that I was already reneging on our deal. I was glad I really didn't know anything more, because I might have looked guilty. But he couldn't expect me to reveal mere speculation on my part that Tilson had been blackmailing Donovan.

"Do you have any other information you haven't told us yet?"

I thought about mentioning that inspectors would soon be crawling all over the murder scene, but decided that wasn't really information about the murder. Sparking an investigation into the housing site had to do with my aesthetic opinion of Donovan's house and my anger with Manning. I didn't think I had to share any of that with the lieutenant.

"Am I still a suspect in the murder of Merv Tilson?" I asked.

Laurence gave the idea lengthy consideration.

"You're not at the top of our list."

"Why not?" I heard a touch of disappointment in my voice. I

guess none of us likes to be rejected from any list.

"Tilson was hit on the head. Hard. Since he was almost six feet tall and the blow came down near the top of his head, we're estimating that the assailant had to be at least five feet eight."

"So for the same reason that I'll never be a high-fashion model, I can't be a murderer?"

"Not in this instance anyway."

That left me out, but I knew that Nick Manning, at six-one or so, would still be a possible suspect.

Laurence left the office a few minutes later, after repeating the terms of our deal and warning me not to violate them. I gave him a firm handshake and a collegial nod, hoping this would buy me enough time to solve the case before he did.

The rest of the morning I spent catching up on Auntie Mabel letters. I sometimes wondered if I was getting any better at it.

Work assiduously at it every day, and you'll soon improve. Auntie Mabel always said that to me when I got down in the dumps. I was certain she had to be right, but I wasn't sure I could see any change for the better. *It takes time to develop a sensitive ear for other people's problems,* Auntie Mabel often reminded me. I agreed but told her I had no intention of spending the rest of my life dispensing free advice, so there was no point in my getting too good at it. *I thought the same thing, too,* she replied, darkening my mood.

It was late afternoon when Mrs. Pear appeared and asked me if I knew anyone named Rhonda Fortier. I said no.

"Well, she's out by my desk and wants to see you."

"What's it pertaining to?"

"She won't say. I warned her that I can't let just anyone into the newsroom. After all, we have to maintain some level of security here. But she still won't talk to me. She says it's confidential and she'll only tell you in person."

Mrs. Pear's newfound emphasis on security came as a surprise to me, since I continually found myself being approached while at my desk by deliverymen, traveling salesmen, solicitors for charitable organizations, and even small children, all of whom apparently walked past Mrs. Pear's desk with impunity. Whether due to her occasional visits to the ladies' room or even more frequent trips outside for a smoke, Mrs. Pear was the most permeable of membranes and hardly the valiant defender of my privacy she was claiming to be.

I told Mrs. Pear to send the woman in. That earned me a withering glare, either because Mrs. Pear wanted to know what this was all about, or because I was allowing a major breach of journalistic security I didn't know. At any rate, she insisted on escorting the woman to my desk. The woman, who repeated that her name was Rhonda Fortier, sat in the chair next to my desk and stared at Mrs. Pear until she walked away. Even after Mrs. Pear was out of earshot, Rhonda's voice was little more than a hoarse whisper.

"I saw your name on the byline for the story about Merv."

"I'm handling that story. Do you have some information?"

"Maybe."

I looked at her expectantly.

"I want something in return," she said.

This seemed to be my day for making deals.

"What?"

"I need to know how much money he left behind."

"Why do you want to know that?"

"Because we lived together, so if he did have any money, it should belong to me."

"Were you married?"

She shook her head.

"Then I'm not sure the law would agree with you."

"Look, I'm not here to talk about the law. I just want what's mine."

"I don't see how I can help you."

"Can't you call the police or somebody and just find out how much he had left?"

I picked up the phone and called Farantello. When I was put through, I asked him Rhonda's question.

"I assume you have a good reason for asking me," he said.

"One that I'd rather keep to myself right now."

"Hang on," he said after a moment's thought.

"He's checking," I said to Rhonda. She didn't nod or smile. She just kept staring at the top of my desk.

Farantello came back on the line. "The inventory shows that he had one hundred and ten dollars and eighty-five cents on him when the body was found."

"What about in his room at the motel?"

"Nothing."

"Thanks. I'll stay in touch."

"See that you do."

I reported the information to Rhonda. Her lips curved into a bitter smile.

"Probably the cops took it."

"What are you talking about?"

I could see her struggling—whether to tell me or not. Finally, she leaned forward, and in a whisper said, "Merv always came home for the weekends. And each week he's been out here, he's been bringing home an extra five thousand. He called it our little nest egg, and we'd go down to the bank on Saturday morning and put it in our savings account."

"Where was the money coming from?" I asked.

"Merv wouldn't tell me. Whenever I asked him, he'd just smile and say everyone has secrets. Another time I wanted to know if he was doing anything that would get us in trouble with the police, and he said that the police would never become involved in something like this."

"Did you talk to him on the phone during the week?"

"Sure, he'd call me, some time every night."

"Did he mention to you whether he'd gotten the five thousand for this week yet?"

Rhonda frowned. "He never told me when he got the money. He'd just show it to me like a big surprise on Saturday when he came home."

"So then, it's possible that he was never given the money this week?"

"I suppose. I was always a little worried about what Merv was doing to get the extra money. He'd been in trouble before. Do you think whatever he was doing got him killed?"

"I don't know. Are you sure he didn't give you any hint as to exactly what he was up to?"

She shook her head. "Merv could be real tight with information when he wanted to be."

"Well, I think you should be happy that you've still got the ten thousand and let it go at that."

"Do you think the police will try to take that away from me?"

"It depends on what Merv did to get it."

She nodded, and by her expression I guessed she was already developing a plan to hide the money.

Rhonda got to her feet and nodded. "Thanks for the help."

I returned the nod. "Thanks for the information."

As I watched her leave the office, I wondered if Max Donovan had realized the blackmail would never stop and decided to put an end to it himself.

CHAPTER 17

Dear Auntie Mabel,

I have a good friend. Let's call her Myrtle. She is a very kind, considerate person in all ways but one: she is always late. It has reached the point where I arrange to meet her a half-hour early because that means she will show up on time. I have mentioned this problem to her in passing, and she always laughs and says that she can't help it. The time just gets away from her. Should I make more of a point of bringing this up to her in a serious way? I don't want to endanger our friendship, but this is starting to bother me.

Bothered

Dear Bothered,

Everyone is late occasionally, and that can be excused. The person who is chronically late, however, is either indicating how little she values the other person's friendship or attempting to assert that she is the dominant person in the relationship. You clearly are not happy with Myrtle's chronic lateness, so I suggest that you mention it to her. Perhaps you might suggest that she select the time when you should meet and tell her that you will wait ten minutes but no more before leaving. If she is still late, then I suggest you find a more punctual friend.

Auntie Mabel

"Who are these people?" Max Donovan finally bellowed. "And

what the hell are they doing on my land?"

He probably would have bellowed sooner, but it had taken him several seconds to catch his breath after performing his lumbering imitation of a sprint from the road where he had parked his car to where Nick and I were standing near the back of the building site. Bibi had called me at the paper and warned me that by ten o'clock, there would be a local EPA team checking out the Donovan site.

Nick held an official-looking document in front of Donovan's face. "According to this, they're from the Ravensford Environmental Protection Commission."

Donovan grabbed the document from Nick's hand and stared at the official letterhead for so long that I wondered if he had lost his ability to read. Then his hand fell to his side and he stared out over his building site. At least fifteen people were walking, burrowing, and climbing on the land, apparently intent on examining every square inch.

"It's like an infestation of gophers," Donovan said with distaste, as if he could happily shoot them all for the vermin they were. "And they're just a bunch of damned kids."

He glanced down on one guy who looked to be about eighteen, sporting a Mohawk and numerous tattoos, who was carefully taking a soil sample from almost under his foot. Donovan reached back with his leg as if to give him a kick, then apparently thought better of it and stepped to one side.

"Most of them are college students from Ravensford's environmental science program. They're working as interns for the EPA," Nick explained.

Donovan studied the scene. "There's got to be someone here of drinking age who's in charge."

"That would be Professor Jenkins. He's the one who gave me the documents," Nick said, pointing to a middle-aged man puffing on a pipe and watching a young woman take a water sample from a small puddle.

Donovan strode over to Jenkins and walked so close, they almost touched.

"What the hell do you think you're doing here?"

The man slowly removed the pipe from between his teeth, took a step back, and gave Donovan a slow onceover.

"I suppose you're the owner of this land. Am I right?" His blue eyes crinkled in an amused expression.

"Of course, you're right. Now I'm asking you: What's going on here? What gives you the authority to trespass on my land?"

"That would be the great and sovereign City of Ravensford. It's all in the papers that I gave your architect. 'Course I realize it takes a while to plow through all that legal gobbledygook. So let me save you the expense of a high-priced lawyer and just say that all those documents are in order."

Donovan stared at Jenkins, slowly turning red in the face, like a small child about to have a temper tantrum.

"I believe that what Mr. Donovan would really like to know is why you are here and what, specifically, you are looking for," I explained.

The man puffed on his pipe and nodded agreeably.

"Let me take the second part of that question first. We are not looking for anything specific. In fact, we are doing a general examination of the land, checking for both soil and water-borne toxins. We are also measuring the slope of the land to try to determine the likelihood of runoff into the Ravensford River. And since we're here, we are also doing a bio-survey to determine what effect, if any, the building will have on indigenous flora and fauna."

"You mean you're looking for some damned endangered species?" Donovan asked, leaning toward Jenkins as though he knew one individual he'd like to endanger.

"You never know what you'll find. Why, I could tell you

stories . . . but I guess this isn't exactly the time or place," the man concluded with an amiable grin.

Donovan balled his hands into fists. Nick stepped between the two men, laying a calming hand on Donovan's shoulder, which he abruptly shook off.

"Professor Jenkins," Nick said, "when we first submitted our request for a permit to build to the town, nothing was said about needing this kind of inspection. Why has the situation changed?"

The professor nodded his head as though that was a reasonable inquiry.

"Usually on single-dwelling requests, the environmental impact is considered to be minimal, and a level-one inspection is adequate. However, if a request for a level-two inspection is filed by someone owning property contiguous with the building site, then we have to act."

"And somebody complained?" Nick asked. "Who?"

"You can check down at the city hall. They have all the local paperwork."

"It must have been Frank Taylor. I'll kill that . . ."

As if on cue, Frank Taylor walked out of his house. He saw me and gave a wave. I waved back weakly.

Donovan's eyes focused on me like a laser.

"Why is he waving at you? What did you have to do with this?"

"I just recommended a lawyer."

"Every man's entitled to good representation," Jenkins said sagely and puffed some more on his pipe.

Donovan's eyes rolled like those of a bull that's been poked once too often by the picadors. He couldn't seem to decide if he wanted to confront Jenkins or me. Finally, he took a step toward Jenkins. In a fight, my money was on the environmentalist, whose arms were roped with muscles and whose gentle demeanor probably concealed a tough character honed by long hikes in the woods. Nick must have decided that a fight was in no one's best interest. He grabbed Max by the arm and pulled him back before he could attack.

"What do think you are doing?" Donovan hissed at him, pulling his arm away.

"Saving you from an assault charge or worse."

Donovan stared at the ground, breathing heavily.

"You're right, Manning. My fight isn't with this old fool. It's with the people who blew the whistle on me." He stared right at me. "You and these damned neighbors who can't accept change. Well, you're all going to be sorry that you tangled with me."

Not saying another word, he stalked off in the direction of his car.

"If I were you, I'd keep track of that fella," Jenkins advised, staring down into the bowl of his pipe. "He doesn't seem quite right in the head to me."

I felt like I should apologize to Nick for being a cause of this inspection. But once Donovan stormed away, he immediately started talking to Jenkins, so I returned to the office and sat behind my desk, feeling guilty. I spent the rest of the morning being Auntie Mabel. She had tried to comfort me with the reminder that if you've done the right thing, there's no reason to feel guilty.

If only life were so simple. I knew that part of the reason I'd turned the EPA loose on Donovan was because I was angry at Nick for the way he treated Ronnie. Now not only did I doubt that I was justified in doing that, but I had to admit to myself that I shared some of his doubts concerning Ronnie's engagement. I'd known my friend long enough to realize that Ronnie was capable of fooling herself into thinking that the briefest of relationships was a solid foundation leading inevitably to a golden wedding anniversary.

I didn't like to admit my doubts about the engagement even to myself, because it seemed more important to Ronnie than any of her other relationships had been. But examined in the cold light of day, neither Ronnie nor Everett showed great potential when it came to the spouse department. On the other hand, they seemed be getting along well so far. Neither had been out of the other's company except for work since they had first met, and there were some indications that both of them were showing more maturity together than they had as individuals. And truth be told, I was a bit relieved that Nick had run his test, because it helped convince me that Ronnie's usually roving eye was a bit more focused than usual.

"You can't go in there. That's private!" I heard Mrs. Pear shout.

A second later Max Donovan's hulking form was planted in front of my desk. Attached to his arm was Mrs. Pear, who was ineffectually trying to drag him back to the lobby.

"I told him absolutely no one was allowed back here without authorization," Mrs. Pear said.

"Let go of me," Donovan said, twisting his arm away from her.

Undaunted, Mrs. Pear seized his other arm and appeared ready to go another round, which I thought might prove dangerous.

"That's all right, Mrs. Pear," I said more calmly than I felt. "You can stop pulling on Mr. Donovan's arm."

Mrs. Pear immediately let go of Donovan's arm as if it were an infected organ and stared hard at him, obviously not intending to leave him alone with me for one second.

"What can I do for you, Mr. Donovan?" I asked.

"You know damned well what you can do. You can tell me why you put these tree-huggers on to me."

"I'm afraid you're exaggerating. As a good neighbor, the

Chronicle simply gave advice to some people who were attempting to exercise their rights."

"That's true," Mrs. Pear threw in, clicking her dentures in Donovan's direction.

"Why don't you go back to your desk, you old biddy?" Donovan said.

Although he was only expressing an opinion I frequently shared, something snapped in me at hearing this gross man express that view. I got to my feet and walked toward him, forgetting for the moment that I more than half suspected him of murder. Out of the corner of my eye, I saw Russ Jones come down the hall. He took one look at what was going on and dove into his office. The coward.

"Mrs. Pear is not an employee of yours to be ordered around at your whim. And if you really wish to know why I helped contact the EPA, it's because your bad taste alone is enough to destroy the environment, regardless of any toxins in the soil."

"Why you little . . ." Donovan began, seizing my arm.

I tried to pull away, but he had a firm grip. I was about to try kicking him where it would do the most good when I saw Mrs. Pear being gently lifted up and moved out of the way. The next thing I saw was Nick Manning grabbing Donovan by the shoulder and slamming him hard against the wall. Max's jaws clicked shut, and a vacant expression came over his face.

"Are you all right, Laura?" Nick asked.

"Perfectly fine," I lied. My arm stung where Donovan had twisted it, and my knees felt a bit shaky. "I could have handled him."

Nick smiled. "Maybe you could have at that, but since I was here anyway, I figured I'd save you the risk of breaking a nail."

I nodded and thanked him for his help.

"You're fired, Manning," Max said hoarsely. He was trying to shout, but didn't seem to be quite able to locate his voice yet.

"I'm not surprised," Nick said. "And I'm just as glad not to be part of your fiasco any longer."

Max grunted, then he looked down the hall.

"I don't know why I bothered with you anyway," he said to me, turning to head down the hall to Wally's office. "You're just a flunky here. My business is with the top man."

"Stop him!" I shouted. I knew Wally wouldn't be happy to have anyone as rowdy as Donovan barge in on him.

Nick ran after him, but it was too late. Max pushed open the door and strode angrily into the office. He had only taken a couple of steps when a large colorful object hit him directly in the face. Stunned, he stumbled to one side and knocked a lamp off the table.

"So sorry, old chap," Wally said, rushing across the room to offer him a hand to steady himself. "I guess I should have shouted 'fore' or something. Although I suppose that isn't quite the done thing in fly fishing. Might scare off the fish."

"What the . . ." Max sputtered, sitting down in a chair and rubbing his forehead, which was slightly red where he'd been hit by the fly.

"Hmm. Looks like you might have a small abrasion there," said Wally, studying Max's forehead with sympathy. "These Patagonian sinkers are rather heavy. Of course they have to be if you're trying to catch the giant Amazonian bass. Some of those lads can get up to twenty pounds. They stay on the bottom of the river, so you really need some weight to get down to them."

Donovan stared at Wally as if he were in the presence of a madman.

"Are you sure you're okay? You seem a bit confused," Wally said. "We can't have subscribers to the *Chronicle* getting hurt in the managing editor's office. You are a subscriber, aren't you?" Wally asked innocently, ignoring my frantically shaking head.

"I am not a subscriber," Donovan shouted. "I'd like to see

this place burned down and plowed over."

"Not a fan of the print medium, I take it?" Wally said.

"You people are incredible. First, you try to get the city to stop me from building my house, and then you pretend you have nothing to do with it."

"Mr. Donovan is the man who is building on the site near the river. The one where the body was found."

"Most unfortunate," Wally said. He stuck out his hand. "Grown men shouldn't let small differences poison their relationships."

Max stared at the offered hand.

"We have no relationship except for the one we'll have in court when I have you brought up on charges for assault and battery."

Wally grinned. "Battery with a fishing fly. That should be unusual enough to make the papers. It might even make the Boston papers. That's where you have your business, isn't it?"

Donovan blanched, probably at the thought of his business cronies in the defense industry reading about his attempt to have an elderly man charged with attacking him with a fishing fly. He'd be the laugh of the health club.

"And it's particularly unfortunate about the Tiffany lamp," Wally continued, looking at the lamp's shattered remains with what could almost be a tear in his eye. "I realize it was an accident, but someone must pay, nonetheless. The insurance company had it covered for thirty thousand, but you know how insurance companies are. They pay up, but then they go after the poor unfortunate who knocked it off the table. So sad."

"You can't threaten me," Donovan muttered through a clenched jaw.

"I wouldn't dream of it, my good fellow. But you must admit that you barged into my office without warning and knocked an expensive antique off the table. I'm afraid that, even under the most generous interpretation possible, things could go badly for you."

Nick caught my eye and smiled. It was refreshing to see Max handled so expertly.

Max straightened his spine and seemed to regain some of his poise.

"You just take me to court, then. But in the meantime, I'm going to get the go-ahead and build my house. And just to show you, I'm going to ask my new architect"—he paused to glance triumphantly at Nick—"if I can add a fourth floor. By the time I get through, people will be identifying Ravensford as the town with the giant chateau."

He turned on his heel and headed for the door, but stopped when he stood in front of Nick.

"You're fired."

"You already told me."

"I don't want you to forget it. And I'm going to tell everyone I know that you're the last person they should hire to design a house. You'll find that I know a lot of people. When I get through with you, you'll be selling doghouses on your front lawn."

"What an irritating man," Wally said when Donovan finally left the room.

"But he has enough money to be dangerous," I pointed out. "I'd take seriously his threat to add a fourth floor to his tower of horrors."

"After the first three, I doubt it will matter," Wally said.

"Do you think the EPA tests will turn up anything to prevent him from building?" Nick asked.

"Hard to tell," I replied.

"What we need is a Plan B to stop him," Wally said. He picked up his fly reel and cast across the room, barely missing me.

"We'd better get out of here before he does some real harm," I said.

"A shame about the lamp, though," Nick added.

"Twenty-nine ninety-nine," I said. "If you want one, I'll sell it to you at wholesale. Good thing our friend Donovan doesn't know any more about lamps than he does about design."

Wally chuckled and sent his Patagonian sinker sailing across the room once again.

CHAPTER 18

Dear Auntie Mabel,

My husband's favorite uncle, Uncle Joe, frequently comes over to visit us. The problem is that whenever my husband isn't around, Joe tries to become overly familiar with me. I've asked him to leave me alone, but he seems to feel that being family gives him certain rights. I told my husband about these events after they happened, but he says that Uncle Joe is just kidding around and I shouldn't take him seriously. What can I do?

Angry and Hurt

Dear Angry,

Whether Uncle Joe is just joking or not, if his attentions are making you uncomfortable, they constitute sexual harassment and he should be made to stop. Since you have voiced your complaints to your husband and he has refused to take them seriously, the next time Uncle Joe becomes overly amorous I suggest that you immediately find your husband and tell him that he has to prevent Uncle Joe from behaving in this way. If your husband still refuses to take you seriously, I suggest you tell him to choose between you and Uncle Joe. Whichever way he chooses, I think you will come out the winner.

Auntie Mabel

"Your boss is quite a guy," Nick said once we were back by my desk.

I nodded. "Don't let that eccentric act fool you. Underneath

153

it is a mind that's pretty shrewd and devious."

There was a long silence, as if we'd run out of words to say, or one of us was expecting something the other wasn't supplying.

"I want to thank you again for coming to my assistance with McDermott. I don't think any man has ever . . ."

"Fought for you before?"

I smiled as I realized that, although I took pride in being able to take care of myself, there was something rather nice in having a man occasionally defend me, especially a handsome man standing very close to me wearing a knit shirt that defined his muscular torso. I cleared my throat.

"I guess I'm accustomed to fighting my own battles."

"And I'm sure you do it very well, but everyone can use a little help once in a while."

"I'm sorry defending me cost you your commission. And now Max is going to start a vendetta against you, and he can be a bad enemy to have. It might ruin your career in the region."

"At least I won't be an architectural whore."

"I am sorry I said that. I know you have to compromise and give the customer some of what they want."

"Right. But I let the line become a little too flexible with Max. Once he began talking about towers, I knew the final structure was going to be a joke I wouldn't want associated with my name. I should have quit on the spot." Nick smiled sadly. "Eventually I would have quit if he hadn't fired me."

"What are you going to do now?"

Nick shrugged. "My career around here hasn't been much to talk about. I'd been thinking of seeing if one of the large Boston firms doing commercial building would be willing to take me on. But with Max blackening my name, I'm not sure that will happen."

"Is commercial the kind of architecture you're interested in doing?"

"Not really, but a guy has to eat. Speaking of which, would you be interested in having dinner with me tonight? Now that I'm no longer the satanic architect, I thought you might consider it."

I shook my head. "Sorry, but I have to cover the meeting of the library board tonight."

Nick gave a mock pout. "You'd rather cover the library board than go out with me?"

"No, but a girl's got to eat, too. And this is just one of the duller parts of the job."

"Okay. But just tell me, are you turning me down because you're still angry about that stunt I pulled with Ronnie and Steve? I'm really sorry I did that, but it seemed right at the time."

"The more I've thought about it, the less angry I've become," I admitted. "In fact, the more I think about it, the more I can see it as something I might have done myself if our positions were reversed. I'm sorry I got so furious with you."

Nick gave a relieved smile. "Good. So then there really is a library board meeting. You're not just saying that because if I were the last man left in the world, you'd still prefer eating alone."

I smiled. Then I'm not sure what happened, whether I moved first or he did. But our faces got closer together and in my imagination I could already feel his lips pressing on mine.

"I'm going out for a smoke now," Mrs. Pear called from her desk. "I'll be back in five minutes."

Nick looked over his shoulder to see if Mrs. Pear was going to walk around the corner and see us. I turned to see if there was any sign of Russ coming out of his office down the hall.

"We'd better stop," I whispered.

Nick smiled. "I guess I got a little carried away."

"That makes two of us. No harm done."

"Then how about reconsidering tonight?"

"Sorry, the library board won't wait."

Nick held up his hand. "Say no more. I can be patient. How about tomorrow night?"

I grinned. "I see exactly how patient you can be."

"Be reasonable, I've known you for four days, and we'd spent most of that time insulting each other. I'd like us to spend a little normal time together just getting acquainted. I'm sure if we talk together like sensible people, all our misunderstandings can be worked out."

He gave me a crooked, little-boy smile, and I felt my heart melt. This wasn't good. I wanted to be alone for a while to sort out my feelings. I didn't want to hurt him, especially right after he saved me from Donovan, but I wasn't sure what I wanted my next step to be. He was my nemesis: the handsome man.

"Shoo, scat," I said, motioning with my hands for him to leave.

"I'll go for now, but like the man said, I shall return."

"Good. That will give me time to repair my defenses."

Nick arched his eyebrow at me and winked.

"Princess, there aren't walls high enough or moats deep enough to keep you from me."

"Out," I said, and smiled to myself as he saluted and disappeared down the hall.

A few minutes later, the door to Russ's office opened. He came out in the hall, carefully looked around, then approached my desk.

"Sorry. I know I wasn't much help a while ago. It's just that I'm really nervous about screwing things up after what happened back in Boston. Getting into a fight is all I'd need to end up unemployed again."

"I understand." I wasn't sure I really did. When some maniac is about to attack a colleague, female or not, it seems to me that worrying about possible publicity is more than a bit cowardly.

"Who was that guy, anyway?"

I explained to Russ about Donovan and the whole environmental thing.

"Bibi did all that for you?" he asked, amazed.

"Yeah. Why so surprised? You recommended her."

"Primarily because I knew she'd work cheap because she's just starting out, but I never thought she'd make this whole thing into such an issue."

"It is already an issue for the people who live in that neighborhood," I said a trifle sharply.

"Yeah, of course. I didn't mean to sound offhand about it. I'm just surprised that Bibi was able to do so much. She seemed rather passive and despondent when I talked with her. I'll have to keep her in mind if I ever need a lawyer. Do you think you'll be able to stop Donovan from building his house?"

"Hard to tell. We've stopped him until the environmental review is over. He just fired his architect, Nick Manning. That was the guy who slammed him against the wall."

"I guessed I missed that part."

Because you were too busy hiding, I thought.

"But it's too soon to tell whether he'll be given the go-ahead to keep working. I have a bad feeling we'll end up with an ugly chateau on that site yet."

"Well, at least you're fighting the good fight," Russ said, doing a fist punch in the air.

"Right," I replied, still thinking his support was too little, too late.

"Are you on duty tonight?" he asked.

I told him about the library board.

"Lucky you," he said, heading toward the front door. "I'll see you in the morning."

As I watched him go, I thought that my rule about not going out with handsome guys needed some revising. Nick and Russ were both handsome, but so different in other ways. I decided my rule should be: don't go out with the wrong handsome guy. But that rule was worth about as much as no rule at all.

It was around nine o'clock at night, and I had just finished typing up my article on the library board meeting that mercifully had ended early. I had been going at it for an hour, reducing my notes to a brief piece that covered all the so-called important information the public had to have. After hitting the key that sent the article to Sam Aaronson's desk, I sat massaging my temples. To relax my eyes, I glanced across the office and almost rubbed my eyes in disbelief. Bibi Grouse was standing there, just around the corner, silently staring at me. I knew I should lock the front door when I was working late by myself, but once again I had forgotten. Although Bibi did look a little spooky standing there and not speaking, I didn't figure she posed a threat.

"Bibi? Did you want to see me about something?" For a moment she was so silent, I almost believed she was a ghost.

She didn't answer me. I twisted nervously in my chair. The thin young woman had on a t-shirt with short sleeves that revealed painfully thin arms, and she was wearing slacks with tapered legs that made her legs appear even more stilt-like.

"Bibi," I said more firmly.

"I just wanted to see you," she finally said.

"Then come closer so I can get a good look at you," I said, pointing to the chair next to my desk. Reluctantly she approached and took a seat.

"How's the environmental analysis coming?" I asked.

"My visit doesn't have anything to do with that."

"Okay. What does it concern?"

"You and Sebastian."

"There is no 'Sebastian and me,' if I understand what you're saying correctly."

Bibi shook her head as if she didn't want to hear that answer. In the distance an ambulance siren wailed as it made its way up the road to the hospital.

"I can tell by the way he looks whenever he says your name. His eyes get kind of dreamy, like they do when he talks about his work. Then he gets this 'little doggy' look, like he'd be willing to jump up and down and beg and fetch if you asked him to."

"I'm sure you're misinterpreting his emotions. He feels gratitude toward me because I offered to write an article about his show, and I got my boss to look at his work. That's all it is. We're friends, nothing more."

"Maybe it's nothing more to you," Bibi said, her face assuming a stubborn pout. "But I'm telling you it means a lot more to him."

"But you're the one he left here with the other day." I didn't add, "with the intention of hopping into bed," although that was my clear impression.

Bibi's face softened into something that resembled a smile. I jumped at the chance.

"See? That proves you're the one Sebastian's actually interested in. I'm hardly anything more than a business associate."

I had pushed too far. Bibi's face hardened again.

"I've known girls like you. You can get any boy you want, so you throw them away when you're through with them like used tissues for someone else to pick up. You're all alike, you cheerleader types."

"I was never a cheerleader," I said automatically. Of course, I had to admit to myself that I had been encouraged to try out by the coach, but standing on the sidelines cheering for boys had never been my idea of putting my talents to their best use.

"Doesn't matter," Bibi insisted. "You've got the looks and that way of strutting around."

"Bibi," I began in a patient voice, "I can't do anything about the way I look. Whether you believe me or not, men do not fall all over me, and I don't go through life expecting them to. I'm sure I've had the same problems with men that you've had."

Bib looked at me shrewdly. "You're probably one of those women who likes to date average guys because they're so overcome with gratitude, they'll do anything for you. You can wrap them right around your little finger and make them dance."

Wow! Where was all this coming from? I thought. I wanted to reply that what Bibi was saying was all nonsense. But then I thought about my decision not to go out with handsome men. I'd told myself it was because handsome men were unreliable, but she could be right. Did I want to have the upper hand in relationships, and was that why I was reluctant to get involved with Nick?

I looked at Bibi, who was leaning on my desk and looking even more miserable than usual under the harsh fluorescent light.

"What do you want me to do about Sebastian?" I asked softly.

She shrugged. "What can you do?"

"I could tell him very firmly that I'm not interested in him except as an artist and a friend."

"A man like Sebastian is motivated by challenges. He'd simply see that as an indication that he should try harder to win you." There was a touch of pride on Bibi's face when she spoke of Sebastian's determination. She really was in love.

"What if I told him that I was in love with another man?"

"Are you?" Bibi asked, raising her eyebrows hopefully.

"No."

"Then he won't be convinced. Sebastian will want a name."

"Tell him I'm in love with Nick Manning."

Bibi frowned. "Why would Sebastian believe that?"

"He knows Nick, and he knows that Nick is interested in me."

"Who is this guy? Some other plain man who begged you for a date?"

"No," I snapped. I was getting tired of this conversation and Bibi's constant insinuations. Whether true or not, no one likes getting hit over the head with another person's perceptions. "He's a very handsome man, and if I were in love with anyone, he'd be the one."

The truth of that statement hit me in the face, too. I hadn't realized it because we'd been so busy fighting over Ronnie and the Donovan house.

"Do you think Sebastian will believe me?" Bibi asked.

"If he doesn't, I'll tell him myself."

"But what good will that do, if you aren't really in love with this guy Nick? Sebastian will find out sooner or later. Then he'll take off after you again."

"Have more confidence in yourself. Sebastian hardly knows me, and I've never given him any sign that I'm interested in him. You'll have plenty of time to convince Sebastian of how you feel about him before he begins to suspect I'm not really in love with Nick."

"Why won't he suspect right away? Sebastian isn't stupid. If you and this Nick aren't going out or anything, won't he guess that maybe all of this is a lie?"

"Okay, okay. I'll talk to Nick and see if we can go out. Is that enough for you?"

"Will he be willing to do that?"

"I'll get him to," I said. That much I was sure of.

"But how will Sebastian know you're going out with Nick?"

I paused for a minute. It was amazing how quickly one thing led to another when you were constructing a web of lies.

"How about this? I'll let you know when and where Nick and I are going on a date, and then you get Sebastian to take you to the same place. Are you a good actress?"

Bibi nodded. "Every lawyer has to be."

"Then act surprised when we all meet. We'll do the whole 'isn't it a small world' routine."

"When are we going to do this?" Bibi persisted.

"I'll try to set it up for tomorrow night, but it will depend on Nick."

Bibi smiled. The expression of joy on her face made her almost beautiful.

"Sorry I gave you such a hard time," she said, "but I just couldn't stand competing with somebody who's so perfect."

"I'm not perfect, and you have a lot to offer, too. Especially if you'd show a bit more self-confidence and try to stay upbeat."

"Well, thanks for coming up with this plan. I only hope that I can convince Sebastian to take me on a date to wherever you're going."

"Use your feminine wiles."

Bibi looked at me doubtfully as she left.

Sometimes even the advice giver can use some advice, Auntie Mabel said to me.

As usual, Auntie Mabel had a good point.

When I got home that evening I decided to call Nick right away about Bibi's plan.

"You want me to what?" Nick said.

"Pretend to love me."

He cleared his throat. "Why would you want me to do that?"

"I don't want you to, Bibi does."

I heard Nick sigh over the phone. "You know, Laura, one of

the things I've come to admire about you on our short acquaintance is your clarity and directness. When you have something to say, you come right out and say it. But this time I'm afraid you've lost me. Who the heck is Bibi, and why should I care what she wants?"

"She's Sebastian Krank's girlfriend, or at least she would like to be."

"Crank!"

"Now, now."

"Okay, his name is Krank. All the same, why should I—or you, for that matter—do anything to help Krank's wannabe girlfriend?"

"Because she's the lawyer who's got Donovan on the run."

"I guess that is a reason to help her. But this sounds bizarre."

"Look, she thinks that Sebastian is infatuated with me, and the only way she can win his heart is by convincing him that I love somebody else."

"He is infatuated with you. A blind man can see that." Nick sighed. "So let me get this straight. We'd go out together and we'd have to pretend to be in love with each other."

" 'Pretend' being the operative word. We would just be putting on an act."

"You mean like the last time when we almost kissed."

"One almost kiss doesn't mean we're in love. But I'll admit I wouldn't even pretend to be in love with someone who was truly reprehensible. You don't quite fit into that category. That's why I suggested the idea to Bibi."

Nick laughed. "You have such a charming way of asking for a favor. 'Not truly reprehensible' is pretty high praise coming from Laura Magee. That's the equivalent for most women of being a male sex god."

"So you're willing to do it."

"Of course, I just want us to have a chance to get to know

each other while we're not fighting over something. I guess if the only way I'll get a date is by playing a part, I haven't got much choice. Where do you think we should go?"

"Why don't we go back to Johnson's Farm, the scene of Ronnie and Everett's announcement? Sebastian thought the place was very romantic. Of course, it is kind of expensive."

"Don't worry, I'll pay my half," Nick offered.

"Your half," I said.

"Well, you certainly didn't expect me to pay for both of us on a pretend date, did you? After all, I'm not much more than a male escort. Maybe you should be paying for both of us."

"Don't push it, Manning." I smiled to myself. Maybe Bibi was right, and I had been looking for men who would do whatever I wanted. It was fun to find one who wouldn't. "The idea of splitting the expenses is fine. In fact, maybe you're right, and I should pay for both of us. After all, it was my idea."

"No, I'll pay the whole thing," he said, sounding embarrassed. "I was only kidding."

"The only problem with Johnson's Farm is that Bibi will have to get Sebastian to take her there. It's not exactly the kind of place that a starving artist and an unemployed lawyer would go. Sebastian might balk at spending so much money."

"Have Bibi tell him that she won some money and wants to take him out."

"Where did she win this money?"

"From you. You'll have to cover the cost of their dinner. I'll pay for ours and you pay for theirs. Seems fair."

"Yeah, I guess it does have a kind of odd fairness to it."

"But to give Krank his due, I don't think he's cheap. After all, he did pay for a second bottle of champagne at Ronnie and Everett's engagement dinner."

"I'll leave it up to Bibi. If she doesn't think Sebastian can afford it, I'll pay for it. If she doesn't like that idea, we'll go somewhere cheaper."

"I'm not at my most romantic over a burger and fries."

"They're okay with me as long as you skip the onions."

CHAPTER 19

Dear Auntie Mabel,

Recently my husband has been insisting that we should prepay our funeral. He wants us to pick the funeral home where we would like to be laid out, purchase our caskets, and pay for everything now. He says it will be cheaper to do it now than in the future and save the remaining spouse money in his or her time of grief. I think the whole idea is morbid. We're only in our sixties, and I for one have a lot of living left to do.

Grossed Out

Dear Grossed Out,

Many people find it difficult to think about their own final arrangements. But your husband does have a point. It will be cheaper to pay now; plus you will have the peace of mind that comes from having one less decision to make. Perhaps, if you really don't want to be involved, you could let your husband take charge of this matter. If you don't trust him to make wise selections, you might choose another family member to accompany him.

Auntie Mabel

The next morning I rolled out of bed a little later than usual. Ronnie was long gone. She had to be at the Lexus dealer by seven-thirty, so she left at six-forty-five. Most of the time I arrived at the paper by eight-thirty, but after putting in a couple of extra hours last night, I didn't see any problem at showing up by nine. There was nothing that wouldn't wait.

A lot of folks must have felt differently.

By the time I arrived, the newspaper parking lot was filled to overflowing with police cars, state emergency vehicles, and television trucks. I had to drive down the street and pull into the parking lot of The Bent Fork, one of my favorite places to have lunch when I wasn't watching my waistline. As soon as I got out of my car, a police officer staggered up, clearly out of breath after his half-block sprint from the newspaper lot.

"What's happened?" I asked.

He ignored my question.

"Ms. Magee," he said between huffs and puffs, "you have to come with me. Lieutenant Laurence wants to talk to you." He had a hand resting on the holster of his gun as if I might be ready to resist.

"Fine. I was only looking for a place to park."

I immediately turned and set off at a fast clip for the crowd scene around the newspaper. I could hear the officer just off my right shoulder struggling along to keep up. I marched right up to Lieutenant Laurence, who was talking to a couple of people in uniform. I saw Michael Farantello off to the side, leaning against his unmarked car and not talking to anybody.

"You needed to see me?" I asked Laurence.

"In just a minute. Be patient," he ordered.

"I think I'll go talk to Lieutenant Farantello then. He probably knows what to ask me."

Laurence gave me an annoyed look. "Don't leave the scene."

I didn't know if that meant I shouldn't move from the spot or that I wasn't to leave on a vacation to the Galapagos Islands. I split the difference and went over to talk to Farantello. Michael looked up as I approached and gave me one of his patented sad smiles. He always looks his most handsome when he's sad; there's just something about those deep brown eyes.

"What's going on here?" I asked, bringing myself back to reality.

"Sam Aaronson showed up for work this morning at six-thirty," Michael said.

"Wow. I always wondered how early he came in. Since he hardly ever leaves before eight at night that's a long day."

"Well, the important event of today is that he found Max Donovan's body behind the dumpster."

"Donovan's dead? How?"

"Hit on the head, just like Tilson."

"What was Sam doing by the dumpster?"

"He says he saw some trash in the parking lot and decided to throw it away."

"Sam really does it all," I marveled. I realized this sounded irrelevant, but I was still trying to process the idea of Donovan being murdered.

"Not everything. We don't think he killed Donovan."

"Of course not. The thought of Sam murdering anyone is ridiculous."

Farantello shrugged. "We gather that Donovan was talking about suing the paper. The paper is pretty much Sam's life, isn't it?"

"Sure, but . . ."

Farantello raised a hand, cutting me off. "Like I said, we don't really think Sam did it. Our best guess is that whoever killed Donovan hit him on the head with a metal instrument of some kind. The blow was up high then down." Farantello demonstrated by raising his hands over his head and bringing them down in front of him. "Sam's got bad bursitis in both shoulders. He can't get his arms over his head."

"When was Donovan killed?"

"The M.E. estimates five to seven hours ago."

"Didn't his wife notice he was missing?"

"She went back to Boston yesterday afternoon. Donovan was staying out here alone. He had a room at the Collins Inn."

"A change from the Sheraton."

Farantello shrugged.

"Why does Laurence want to talk to me so badly?"

Farantello gave me a slow smile. "Take your best guess."

"He heard about the fight I had with Donovan in the newspaper office yesterday."

"More than heard about it. Mrs. Pear gave him a rather dramatic reenactment. The only question left is whether you killed him or Manning killed him, or you were in it together."

I felt a little sick to my stomach, but knew that I had to brazen it out. "C'mon, if I had killed the guy, why would I have dumped him in the newspaper parking lot? I'd heave him into the Ravensford River or drag him out in the woods somewhere."

Farantello smiled. "It's good to know your methods for the investigation of our next murder in town."

"Get real!" I snapped. "What motive did I have to kill the guy?"

"According to Mrs. Pear, he was threatening to sue the paper, and Wally and you personally, by the time he was through."

"The newspaper would cover me in any lawsuit of that kind."

"Maybe. But even Roger St. Clair might fire you if it was a choice between you and saving the paper."

"Phooey!"

"Okay. Let's say that for old time's sake I think you're innocent. What about Manning? He'd just been fired by the guy; twice, according to Mrs. Pear."

Mrs. Pear's attention to details was impressive. It was hopeless to warn her not to say much to the police. She'd fix me with her bleak smoker's squint and tell me that not telling the complete truth wasn't much different from a lie.

"Manning didn't want to build Donovan's house. He was glad to be fired."

"But he wouldn't have been happy to have Donovan going around the state saying what an incompetent architect he was."

I didn't have a response to that. "I don't think he'd kill him over that," I said lamely.

Before Farantello could respond, Lieutenant Laurence appeared at my side. I could see he was ready to pepper me with questions. I was glad to have had the rehearsal with Farantello.

Two hours later, I was finally through being asked basically the same questions and giving the same answers to several different people in both state and local uniforms. What I had discovered was that there was no evidence linking me to the murder; however, I did have motive and opportunity. Mrs. Pear's Tolstoy-like commentary had provided the motive, and the fact that I sleep alone, or at least slept alone last night, left me with the opportunity. Fortunately, there was no circumstantial evidence linking me to the crime, so far at least. And since Max had been hit on the head like Tilson and was about the same height, I was off the hook because of shortness. From what I overheard, I knew they also had a team interrogating Nick, who wouldn't catch the same break.

"Multimillionaires are a dime a dozen, honey," Mrs. Pear was informing Ronnie as I came into the office. I wondered what Ronnie was doing here on her lunch break and hoped there wasn't some new problem to deal with, since I hadn't fully adjusted to almost being a possible murder suspect yet again.

"It's not just what they've got in their wallets that counts," Mrs. Pear announced loudly enough to be heard across a football stadium. "What they've got in front matters more."

Ronnie looked bewildered for a moment. When Mrs. Pear pointed to her groin, Ronnie blushed. Ronnie never blushed when it came to sex, but maybe getting the facts from someone old enough to be your grandmother and with a voice like a megaphone was hard for even Ronnie to take.

"Now Mr. Pear was a man with more than his normal share of natural endowments, if you get what I mean. Why, his equipment . . ." She held her hands so far apart that Ronnie's eyes grew wide with amazement.

"Did you come to see me, Ronnie?" I asked before the public description of Mr. Pear's privates became even more detailed.

Ronnie glanced at me, but seemed reluctant to leave when her conversation with Mrs. Pear was at such a high point, so to speak.

"Let's go, then," I said, pulling on her arm until she reluctantly waved goodbye to Mrs. Pear who, cigarettes in hand, headed outdoors.

"What is it?" I asked when Ronnie was finally settled in the chair next to my desk.

"Somebody said that Max Donovan was found murdered right outside?"

I nodded.

"That's terrible. I know he wasn't a very nice man, but . . ."

"It's worse than that," I said and filled her in on how Nick and I were at the head of the suspects list.

"Oh, God, I hope you can stay out of jail until tomorrow."

"Why is tomorrow so important?"

"Everett and I were thinking about having a little barbecue at lunch time out at the cottage, and we were hoping that you could come."

"If I'm not in the slammer by then, I'll make the effort."

If I worked on Auntie Mabel all afternoon, I'd be far enough ahead to take the afternoon off.

"Don't you have to work tomorrow?" I asked Ronnie.

"My boss shifted the schedules around when I told him I had something important to do."

I'll just bet he did, I thought.

Ronnie sat there chewing her lip, a signal that she had more to say and was nervous about saying it.

"Everett thought it would be nice if Nick came along, too. I know you don't get along that well, but he is Everett's best friend. And Mrs. Pear told me that Nick knocked Max Donovan down yesterday, so I thought that might make you like him better now."

"Nick knocked Donovan down when he tried to manhandle me."

"He did?" Ronnie's eyes grew large. "How romantic! Why that's just like something you'd see in the movies."

"Yeah, but his timing was lousy," I said and explained how it had made us both murder suspects.

Ronnie waved her hand. "Don't worry. Nobody would ever believe that you or Nick could have murdered that detestable man. He must have had lots of enemies."

"I hope so. And I hope that most of them were in Ravensford last night."

"So will you come?" Ronnie asked, not to be deterred from her important mission.

"I'll be happy to come."

"Goody!"

"But on one condition."

"What's that?"

"I'd like to invite Sebastian Krank and Bibi Grouse."

"Who's Bibi Grouse?"

I explained and gave her a summary of the plan to convince Sebastian that I was in love with Nick.

"Invite them. That's great. I think you and Nick are swell together. Even though he doesn't like me, I think he's just the right guy for you."

"We're only pretending to be in love, Ronnie," I reminded her.

"The only reason he doesn't like me is that he thinks I'm not right for Everett, but I hope that someday he'll change his mind," Ronnie continued, ignoring my correction.

I sighed. Sometimes there really was no point in talking to Ronnie.

"So I'll see you tomorrow at the cottage," Ronnie said, standing up.

"Fine. I've still got your upside-down directions in case I get lost."

Ronnie took a few steps then stopped and turned toward me.

"You know, sometimes pretending can lead to the real thing," she said.

Before I could respond with a resounding denial, she walked away.

"Yeah, and sometimes pretending leads to nothing at all," I said loudly to the empty room as I punched the number for Antic Antiques into the phone.

When Bibi's aunt answered I asked for Bibi. It was quite a while before the lawyer came to the phone.

"You know what she's got me doing today?" Bibi said, then paused as if really expecting me to make a guess.

"What?" I asked dutifully.

"Beating rugs. She's got this thing that looks like something you'd play cricket with, and she's got me outside beating the stuffing out of these rugs she's had stored in the attic since Noah studied the plans for the ark."

"Sounds like filthy work."

"Some of these rugs are older than my aunt, and that's saying something. The only thing holding them together is dirt. If I hit them one more time," she said, her voice rising as if she wanted her aunt to hear, "they're going to fall apart like a mummy's wrappings."

Enough was enough. Time to get to the point. "I called to tell you that Nick and I have a phony date arranged for tonight."

"Fast work," Bibi commented. I thought I could hear a twinge of envy in her voice. "I guess you didn't have any trouble selling him on the idea of pretending to be your boyfriend."

"Not much. We're going to Johnson's Farm. Our reservation is for seven. Sebastian knows where it is. He was there with us the other night when our friends Ronnie and Everett announced their engagement."

"Yeah, Sebastian told me about them. His eyes got all misty when he talked about it. The guy is a real romantic."

"Well, let's hope his pocketbook matches his love of romance because this place is kind of expensive."

"I'll split the cost with him."

"Or you could claim to have won some money and offer to pay the whole thing. I'll pay you back."

"Why would you do that?"

"I want this to work out for you." I didn't think it polite to tell her that having a lovesick Sebastian following me around was the last thing I wanted.

"I'll work it out somehow."

"When you get there, make sure that somehow Sebastian sees Nick and me."

"I'll make our reservation for seven-thirty, and if we can't see you from our table, I'll go to the ladies' room and come back and tell him I saw the two of you, and we should go over and say hello."

"Good."

There was a long pause. "I do appreciate all the help you're giving me."

"Don't mention it. And if you can make it, I'd like to invite you to a barbecue tomorrow at Everett's cottage in the Berkshires. Nick and I will be there, so it will be another chance to put our plot into action."

"Can you and Nick keep up the pretense for a whole afternoon?"

"I don't think we'll have to do anything other than be polite to each other. We can both manage that."

"Okay."

"Sebastian's been out there, so he knows the way."

"After all the help you've given me, I wish I could give you some good news as well, but I'm afraid I can't."

"You've already heard from the Ravensford Environmental Protection Commission?"

"Professor Jenkins called me last night, right after he called Donovan. It's only a very preliminary report. But so far the property is looking as pure as driven snow. No signs of toxins, and the land doesn't appear to be the habitat of any endangered species. The chances of runoff into the river are also minimal. The scientists have some complicated formula based on the distance from the water and the angle of the slope. Based on that, the house will easily be within the margin of safety."

"I guess it really doesn't matter now."

"Why's that?"

"Haven't you heard? Donovan was found dead this morning, murdered."

"You're kidding me."

"Nick Manning and I are currently their two prime suspects."

"Uh, criminal law isn't really my thing. You might want someone with a little more experience."

Yeah, like Perry Mason, I thought.

"You can send your bill to me. If I can't pay it all at once, I'll let you have it on installments."

"No need. Frank Taylor offered to pay whatever it cost. There's one guy who will be happy to see Donovan dead."

"I guess that's true," I said. I wondered if there was some way I could direct Lieutenant Laurence's attention toward Frank and away from Nick and me.

"Oh, one other thing, though like you said, I guess it doesn't matter now. But Donovan told Jenkins he wasn't sure he was going to go ahead with building the house anyway."

"Why?"

"He said all the bad publicity had made him lose interest."

After hanging up, I sat and stared across the empty newsroom. The newsroom had always been a mystery to me. There were at least six desks and none, other than mine, were ever used. Russ and Joy Pleasant, who handled weddings, funerals, and all the social events in between, had small offices down the hall next to Sam Aaronson's, while I sat here like the last remaining vestige of the golden age of journalism. I imagined a time when all these desks were occupied by hard-working and hard-drinking men like you used to see in the movies of the twenties and thirties, the air blue with cigarette smoke and salty language.

Although I had never aspired to be a journalist, even my heart beat a little faster at the thought of what life had been like back then. Oh sure, the *Ravensford Chronicle* had never been a major metropolitan newspaper, but even here there had been a time when the printed word was how people communicated the news of the day, and to be in the newspaper was proof of fame or infamy. Proof that could be kept and passed down from generation to generation on increasingly yellowed sheets of newsprint. A brief spot on the local news that few people could precisely recall a week later had now replaced all of this.

It was enough to make even an old agony columnist like me, who had seen and heard it all, feel a little sad. I looked down at my bag of letters, but couldn't seem to get my hand to reach down and take one out.

When I had that problem I used to treat myself to a little distrac-

tion. Why don't you do that? Auntie Mabel suggested.

I decided that was a good idea and walked down the hall to Wally's office. Maybe I could get his take on the Donovan murder, assuming he'd heard about it. If not, he certainly had to be notified on a matter as important as this one.

A muffled voice invited me to come in. I opened the door with one hand in front of my face to ward off any wayward lures sailing across the room. But Wally wasn't casting; today he was sitting at his corner workbench bent over something. A palette of oil paints was spread out next to him, and as I drew closer, I could see that he was painting what looked to be a statue.

"What's that you're working on?" I asked, not quite able to make out the figure that was shielded by Wally's body.

He leaned back. "A duck. Actually a duck decoy."

I could now see that he had a large photograph of a duck pinned to the table next to him, and was carefully painting a carved wooden replica of one.

"You're making your own duck decoy?"

He nodded. "A hunter friend of mine got me interested."

"Are you planning to take up hunting the same way you took up fly fishing?" I asked. The thought of shotgun pellets ricocheting around the office was too unnerving to contemplate.

Wally smiled and gave my hand a pat.

"You worry too much, my dear."

"I've got reasons to worry."

"Ah, you mean because of Mr. Donovan being discovered in the parking lot this morning after your little altercation with him yesterday."

"Yes. So you knew about the murder."

Wally smiled. "I appear much more disconnected from things than I actually am." He took up some green paint on his brush and bent over the head of the duck. "I found this photo of a rather rare breed of duck from northern California, so I thought I'd try to create a credible decoy. There are decoy competitions. Did you know that?"

I shook my head.

"I wouldn't worry unduly about Mr. Donovan's demise. From our brief acquaintance, he struck me as a man who made many enemies. So before long there will be a host of suspects."

"Any idea who did it?" I asked with a smile.

Wally took my question seriously, his brush staying poised over the duck for several seconds.

"All I can say is that you should avoid being fooled by decoys," he said, and then he chuckled.

Some help.

I went back to my desk and still couldn't seem to get my hand in the bag. I felt uncomfortable about my date with Nick. I'd thought my rule against dating handsome men was firm and that somehow it was going to be the more sensible road toward successful personal relationships. And here I was violating it less than six months after making it. Why was I doing it?

Oh, I know, it was partly because I felt a little sorry for Bibi and Sebastian, two people who in their own odd way seemed made for each other. And I certainly didn't want Sebastian following me around with calf eyes for months, although I still thought that Bibi was exaggerating the degree of Sebastian's infatuation. But there was more to it than that. Although Nick had been reluctant at first to abandon the Donovan project, he had chosen me over his career when he protected me from Donovan. His attitude toward Ronnie was still mixed, and he had engaged in that prank to test her faithfulness, but didn't that just show his loyalty to Everett? And he had agreed to take part in my little plot to deceive Sebastian.

So why wasn't I enthusiastically leaping at the opportunity to go out with him? The chemistry was clearly there on both sides, so why the hesitation? Was it just residual fear based on my past bad experiences? Or was there something more? On some subconscious level had I picked up a sign that Nick was not all he seemed to be? Or was I simply afraid to go out with a man who challenged me as much as I challenged him?

Whatever the reason, I wasn't ready to completely relax my guard. Our dating was going to remain an act until I felt more confident about Nick. After all, this would be an ideal way to get to know him without actually committing, I thought with a smile.

Auntie Mabel stepped in and interrupted my thoughts. *Sometimes, my dear, you are just far too smart for your own good.*

CHAPTER 20

Dear Auntie Mabel,

My husband is an inveterate liar. At social events I've heard him lie to people about his income, his weight, his education, and the places he's visited. When I call him on it later, he says that there's no law saying he has to tell people the truth and he's just "goofing around." Aside from the embarrassment I experience sitting there while he makes up stories, I am also nervous that someday his storytelling will get him in trouble. What should I do?

Truthfully Worried

Dear Truthful,

Compulsive lying can be a sign of a mental illness. I would recommend that you urge him to seek professional help. If he refuses, I think you should tell him that you will no longer attend social events with him, and that's no lie!

Auntie Mabel

The next morning at the office everything seemed better. There was good reason for me to feel that way: I'd had a good night's sleep; the sun was shining; and I'd just knocked out five Auntie Mabel letters without once becoming sarcastic.

The fact that Mrs. Pear was out this morning made work all the easier because there was no one to tell me stories about the bad behavior of people in the entertainment industry. Mrs. Pear was a treasure trove of such information based on the numerous soft news shows she watched nightly and the tabloids she read daily. But her absence did mean that I had to handle the front counter. I heard the front door open and hurried from my desk to see who was there.

Victoria Donovan stood at the counter with a piece of paper in one well-manicured hand and an impatient expression on her face. I said hello and told her how sorry I was about Max. She nodded and thanked me politely.

"I'd like to have this run in the paper today—tomorrow at the latest."

I read over what she had handed me. It was Max Donovan's obituary. I skimmed the information about his life and focused on the fact that his funeral was to be in Boston in two days.

"We can have it in this afternoon's paper. The obituaries always go to press last."

"Thank you."

"We might want to send someone out to the funeral. Where will it be held?"

"It's private," she snapped. Then she put a hand to her brow. "Sorry. This is a difficult time. If you decide to send someone give me a call." She recited her cell phone number. "We just don't want this turning into a media circus."

"Will you still be building the house?" I asked. I know it sounded a bit self-centered to be asking the grieving widow about something that concerned me, but I really wanted to know.

She shook her head. "That was Max's baby. He was the one who wanted to have a place back in the town where he grew up."

"Did he still have a lot of friends from his days here?"

"I don't think so. But Max liked to impress people. He would have been happy just to have the guy who sat in front of him in third grade look at the house and think about how far Max had come."

"I got the idea from Max that you were the one who wanted a place out here."

She smiled sadly. "One of the tricks to living with Max was that you had to guess what he wanted before he realized it himself, then say it was what you wanted."

"Are you going to take over running his company?"

"No. I'll inherit a controlling interest, but I don't want to be involved in the business. That was Max's pride and joy, not mine. I'll probably sell out. I don't need the headaches."

"According to what I've heard, your husband decided not to build the house after he was pretty much guaranteed that he'd get permission. I wonder why."

Victoria Donovan shrugged. "Max was nothing if not inconsistent when it came to his private life. He'd get passionate about something then suddenly change his mind. It was exhausting keeping up with him."

"So you don't know why he changed his mind about building the house?"

"Sorry."

"Will you be staying in town long?"

"I'll be leaving this afternoon."

Before I could ask any more questions, she stuck out her hand and shook mine, thanked me for my help, and said goodbye.

I went over to my desk and typed up the obituary then fired it off to Sam. Normally that was a job for Mrs. Pear, but I wanted to make sure that it got into today's paper as I'd promised. When I was done I sat there for a moment, thinking about what Nick had mentioned back at Everett and Ronnie's engagement dinner about Everett needing a pre-nuptial agreement. According to his obituary, Max had founded his company over twenty years ago when he was married to his first wife, who had died. He had no children and had married the current Mrs. Donovan only six years ago. All this made me wonder if he had required her to sign a pre-nuptial. I couldn't see Donovan allowing her to sue for divorce and take a big chunk of his company. I decided that I'd have a talk with Bibi to find out what sorts of things usually went into pre-nuptials.

Russ Jones came in the back door. He waved and was about to go into his office when he turned and headed for my desk.

"How did you make out with the police yesterday? I'm sorry I had to tell them about the fight Nick Manning had with Donovan."

"It didn't matter. Mrs. Pear spilled the beans anyway."

"The police don't think you had anything to do with Donovan's murder, do they?"

"Lieutenant Laurence would probably like that, but I think I'm off the hook for the moment."

"What about Manning?"

"I don't know what happened. I tried to call him last night, but his machine picked up. I think I'll give him a call in a few minutes."

"He seems like a nice guy. He certainly stuck up for you when I didn't."

"Don't beat yourself up over it, Russ. You had a good reason not to get involved."

"I suppose."

"Do you know anything about pre-nuptial agreements?"

Russ laughed. "I've never even been married. Why?"

"I was just wondering if the Donovans had one."

"Why is that important?"

"I'm looking for motive. If Victoria would have lost a lot of money by divorcing Max, she might have found another way to end their marriage."

"Do you have any reason to believe that they weren't happily married?" Russ asked.

"Nothing other than the fact that I can't imagine any woman getting along very well with Donovan."

"I'll grant you that," Russ said, giving me one of his stunning smiles. "From what little I saw that day in the office, he certainly didn't seem like one of nature's noblemen. But one thing I've learned over the years is that there's no way of figuring what women want in a man. Maybe Mrs. Donovan thought the sun rose and set on him. People are different."

After I agreed with that, Russ went back to his office. I picked up the phone and called Manning. He answered right away.

"Where have you been, Manning? I thought you might have left the country when I couldn't get you all last night."

"A tempting thought. I turned the ringer off and switched my phone over to voice mail after I got a call from a reporter at the *Herald,* who wanted my reactions to being an accused murderer. I figured that I didn't have to deal with that."

"You weren't actually accused, were you?"

"Not really."

"What *did* the police say?"

"They asked me a lot of questions about why Donovan and I got into a fight. They wanted to know all about the house, and the conflicts I'd had with Max over it. But they particularly wanted to know where I was last night and if anyone could vouch for me."

"What did you tell them?"

"I said that aside from the three blonds who shared the bed with me, there was no one I could think of."

"Very funny."

"Sad, really. I was starting to wish that someone actually had shared my lonely bachelor bed last night and could be my alibi. No such luck."

"Me either."

"We both sound pretty pathetic when it comes to the relationships department. Anyway, the police weren't happy, but I guess they have no evidence that I was involved in the murder. They just warned me not to take any long trips."

"Are you still on for our dinner tonight?"

"Our mock date, you mean? I wouldn't miss it."

"It's all arranged. Bibi and Sebastian will be there."

"I'm not going to have to eat dinner with Krank, am I?"

"Not unless you invite him to share our table."

"That's not happening."

"I made a reservation for seven at Johnson's."

"Where should I pick you up?"

"Why don't we meet at the restaurant?"

Nick snorted. "Doesn't sound much like a date to me."

"Don't worry. Sebastian won't know that we arrived separately. The important thing is that we put on a convincing performance once we're inside the restaurant."

"I'm up for it. Are you?" Manning asked.

I sighed to myself, wondering what I was getting into.

"I'll give it my best shot," I replied.

CHAPTER 21

Dear Auntie Mabel,

My brother-in-law is a drug addict. He has been in and out of rehab for a number of years. My husband thinks that if his brother lived with us he would be more likely to kick his habit because he would have a supportive family around him. I think this is a bad idea, but I can't tell my husband, because it would hurt his feelings and force him to choose between his brother and me. What should I do?

At Wits End

Dear Wits End,

Your brother-in-law belongs in rehab, and your husband should be making every effort to get him back into a program that will help him. Taking him into your home will only enable him to continue to use drugs, and he will soon be "borrowing" money from you to support his habit. Tell your husband this is the time for some tough love.

Auntie Mabel

I looked across the table at Nick, fascinated by the little lines that formed next to his eyes as he smiled at his own foolishness. We'd been sitting for several minutes at our table in the restaurant, talking about our lives, having slipped quite naturally and without any embarrassment into the kind of conversation people might have on a first date. Nick was telling me about his first job as an architect when he had used all of his vast theoretical knowledge of contemporary design to build a barn for a farmer in southern Vermont, only to discover that he had designed doorways too narrow for cows to enter except in single file.

"The old farmer was pretty crusty, but all he said is that cows are like people. They don't like to wait in long lines."

I smiled. I was more impressed by the fact that Nick would tell a story about himself that made him look less than perfect than by the story itself. Here was a handsome man, and he was definitely handsome if the fawning behavior of our waitress was to be believed, who didn't seem to be vain, an unusual combination in my experience.

"Were either of your parents architects?" I asked.

"Nope. Mom is a lawyer and Dad is an anthropologist."

"That must have made for interesting conversation around the dinner table."

Nick's face clouded. "We weren't really around the same table all that much. Mom worked long hours, so Dad and I usually had supper alone together during the school year. Summers Dad would go off to study a small branch of the Shoshone out in Wyoming, so Mom and I would be left alone together."

"Did you have any brothers and sisters?"

He shook his head. "I was the sole beneficiary of a very verbal household. Dad liked nothing better than to chat about his work with me, and Mom was always arguing over the finer points of law. They just didn't talk very much to each other."

Nick paused and shook his head. "Looking back on it all, I often wonder why they stayed together. I suppose that at one time they must have loved each other, but they certainly never seemed to have much in common."

"Other than you."

"Yeah. But I don't think this was a case of staying together

187

for the sake of the child. They had worked out a living arrangement where they each went their own way. They were civil, even
friendly, when they were together, but it was more like two
people sharing a house and a son than being a family. That's
pretty much the way they still live now, like long-term roommates."

"So your mother probably wasn't the baking-cookies-and-
pies-in-the-kitchen-type?"

Nick laughed at the thought. "That was more my Dad's thing,
although he was more likely to try to concoct some ancient Native American food from a recipe he'd gotten from a tribal sha-
man. Mom was more into take-out from a French restaurant.
Neither one fit really well into the traditional gender roles. What
about your mom?"

"She's a teacher. Second grade."

"Does she like it?"

"She loves it. She thinks the kids that age are great. One of
her big regrets in life is that my sister and I grew up. I still don't
think she fully accepts it."

"What about your father?"

"He's in insurance. He works at corporate headquarters. All
he ever says about it is that he moves paper from one side of his
desk to the other. But I think there's more to it than that. He's
a division manager."

"A pretty normal family."

"Very normal. Some of my happiest childhood memories are
of the times my sister and I spent in the kitchen with my mother
learning how to bake."

"Sounds nice."

"It was. Although I will admit that as I got older there were
times I wished my home life was a little less normal. So many of
my friends came from broken or at least badly divided homes, I
began to feel that if my parents at least had big fights once in a

while, it might make me more interesting. I thought suffering would give me a more soulful personality."

"So where did this distrust of men come from?"

"I don't distrust men," I snapped. "I've learned to be cautious."

Nick held up his hands in a gesture of surrender. "Okay, where did all this caution come from then?"

"I brought it on myself. I worked in Boston for five years, at the Boston Museum of Art, as a writer. I also wrote on the side for a couple of small art publications. So most of the guys I went out with were artists, handsome guys with the moral character of gerbils. Some just went out with me because of my connections; others lacked any sense of faithfulness except to themselves. I won't go into it, but some similar things happened here in town. I've finally gotten wise in my old age."

"So handsome guys are guilty until proven innocent because you've had some bad experiences. Isn't that a little simplistic?"

I leaned across the table and looked Nick in the eye.

"I'll bet most of the women in your life have been fluffy little things who wanted nothing more than to cook and clean their way into your heart."

Nick leaned back in his chair, surprise showing on his face.

I arched an eyebrow in triumph.

"Some men marry their mothers; others spend their lives avoiding them. I bet you're in the second category. Sometimes the simple explanation is the right one."

Nick managed a weak grin. "Fair enough. Let's just say that a number of women in my past have been domestically oriented."

"So why aren't you married to one of them?"

Before Nick could answer, Bibi appeared in the periphery of my vision, peering out from behind the dessert cart. She saw the two of us and gave a high sign.

"I have a feeling that we may have company in another minute or two," Nick said, spotting her, too, "so make sure you act nice."

"Make sure I act nice!" I said, loudly enough to attract a stare from the startled couple at a nearby table.

"You see?" Nick said in a tone dripping with patience. "That's what I mean. We're supposed to be in love, not engaged in mortal combat."

He reached across the table and took my hand. I slipped my hand out and grabbed his in a bone-crushing grip. Nick gritted his teeth.

"Remember," he said, "I'm doing this for you."

I loosened my grip and tried to look contrite.

"Here comes Krank now," Nick warned.

Sebastian marched up to our table with Bibi pumping her short, thin legs to keep up with him.

"Laura," he said, giving me a bow, "how nice to see you again." He turned to Nick and gave him a curt nod.

"Hi," Bibi said, trying to edge into the conversation.

Sebastian cleared his throat and turned to me. "I did not realize that you and Mr. Manning were such close friends."

"It was rather sudden," I replied, casting my eyes down and hoping I was giving a convincing imitation of a woman reluctant to admit the depth of her attachment.

"It took us a while to discover how much we had in common," Nick said. He gave me an adoring smile. "Once we did . . . well, we knew that we were made for each other."

Sebastian stared, as if wondering whether he was suffering from auditory hallucinations. Then he turned to me with an expectant expression on his face, hoping I'd deny the whole thing. When I said nothing, he appeared crestfallen.

"Well, I think the two of you make a lovely couple," Bibi threw in with an excess of enthusiasm.

Sebastian gawked at her, as if amazed that he should be dating an idiot. Then he visibly pulled himself together.

"The ways of love are . . ."—he stopped, uncertain how to proceed—"truly mysterious."

"I couldn't agree with you more, Krank. Who would have thought that a classy lady like this would ever give the time of day to a broken-down jock like me. But when that certain chemistry is there, it just can't be denied."

Slowly, gently, Nick raised my palm to his lips and kissed it, all the while looking deep into my eyes.

"Ah," said Sebastian, beaming. "I see that what you say is true, Manning. You do indeed love her."

My palm still tingled as I struggled to get my voice back.

"We've just started going out," I said quickly, pulling my hand back. "I wouldn't exactly say that we're in love yet."

Sebastian laughed. "He is certainly in love with you. I am never wrong about such things."

"You aren't?" I said weakly.

"Never," Sebastian said with confidence. He put his arm around Bibi. "Perhaps, my little sparrow, we should return to our own little nest and leave these lovebirds to theirs."

"Of course, darling," she replied, giving me a triumphant wink.

"All in all, I think that went quite well," Nick said after Sebastian and Bibi had left the room. "Sorry I sounded so unpolished there at the end, but I knew that was Sebastian's opinion of me. He thinks I'm a mere boorish jock, so I had to stay in character. He would never have found me convincing if I suddenly acted like the suave, sensitive guy I really am."

Nick searched my face for a smile. But I wasn't finding anything funny at the moment.

"Do you really love me?" I asked.

"Madly," he said.

I stared at him a moment to see if he was joking. But his face remained serious and his eyes didn't leave my own.

I sank back in the seat feeling like I'd been shoved.

Nick smiled grimly. "A guy usually hopes for a more enthusiastic response to his protestations of love."

"How long have you felt this way?" I asked. I knew I sounded like a doctor trying to assess the stage of a disease, but this had thrown me off balance.

"Since you threw yourself into my arms in Everett's parking lot."

"That was an accident."

"Even accidents can start fires."

"Be reasonable."

Nick shrugged. "Hey, I didn't ask to fall for an attractive, intelligent woman with more quills than a porcupine. Sometimes these things are beyond rational control. If you want me to walk away and leave you alone right now, I'll do it. I'll tell the hostess I've been called away on an emergency and pay for our food. You can take it home with you. Maybe you and Bibi can share a feast over some girl talk. At least she has something to celebrate."

"You can't walk out now. Sebastian might notice and suspect something was wrong between us. We can't give him any reason to think he has a chance with me until Bibi has firmly won him over. Believe me, if I could, I'd walk out right alongside you."

"Why?"

"What do you mean, why?"

"Do you find me so unappealing that the very thought that I love you is enough to send you running out into the night? I know I'm probably not as sophisticated as some of those artsy types you went out with in Boston, but my table manners aren't appalling and I have decent personal hygiene. Just tell me that you don't find me the least bit attractive, and I'll leave. I'll even stop by Sebastian's table to tell him and Bibi I have a family emergency, and could you please join them."

I looked down at my napkin, which was twisted between my hands as if I were trying to throttle it.

"I don't find you unappealing," I said finally without looking up.

"Then what's the problem?"

"This is so sudden. I'm afraid."

Nick nodded as if that were the most natural thing in the world.

"I see our food is coming. Why don't we eat while I tell you about the most frightening moment of my life? Wait, let me begin with the first frightening moment of my life, when I fell out of a tree house at the age of eight."

While I ate, first barely able to swallow the food, Nick went from story to story, most of them dealing with the subject of fear. He ordered a bottle of wine and kept my glass filled up. Gradually I found myself listening to him, not following all the words, but soothed by the rhythm of his voice. And slowly my fear began to lessen. The tightness in my chest eased, and when I glanced down at the table and saw my empty dessert plate, I realized that, as if in a trance, I had just eaten a very large meal. Listening to Nick might be good for the soul, but it could prove hazardous to the waistline.

"Are you ready to go?" Nick asked me. I forced my mind to focus and nodded. "I seem to have done most of the talking," Nick continued. "I hope I wasn't too boring. Next time it's your turn."

I smiled and nodded.

As we waited by the restaurant's entrance for the valet to bring our cars around, Nick leaned over and whispered in my ear.

"Are you less afraid?"

My first reaction was to deny ever having been afraid, but

then I remembered I had already admitted my fear to him.

"I'm less afraid," I admitted.

"Good." Nick looked across the driveway at the darkness gathering over the gardens surrounding the Farmhouse. "Look, it's true that I love you. I'm not sure why, and maybe I never would have admitted it even to myself except for Krank. Whoever thought I'd end up owing that guy anything? But just because I love you doesn't mean you love me. I understand that. And I don't want to frighten you. All I'm asking is that we keep on with our little charade for a while longer and see if there's any chance it will become reality. After all, we can't suddenly stop seeing each other after that big buildup we gave Bibi and Sebastian."

I must have looked doubtful because he asked me again if I was still afraid.

"A little," I admitted.

"People aren't frightened when they're only fooling around. Maybe this is a sign that you have some feelings for me, too."

The valet pulled up with my car.

"I have to go now," I said.

"Sure, but we have to keep up appearances."

I felt myself almost swept off my feet by powerful arms as Nick pulled me to himself and gave me a long kiss. I felt all my tension melt away and relaxed into his arms. Much too soon, it seemed to me, the moment was over.

"See you tomorrow at Everett's," Nick said.

"Right," I mumbled, and found that I was definitely looking forward to it.

CHAPTER 22

Dear Auntie Mabel,

The other night my neighbor obviously had a party. Cars were parked up and down the street and there was loud music playing late into the night. But when I saw him this morning and asked what he'd been celebrating at the party, he pretended not to know what I was talking about. Don't you think that is very rude behavior?

Offended in Ravensford

Dear Offended,

There are a number of possible reasons your neighbor didn't wish to discuss his party with you. Perhaps the party was for a personal reason that he didn't want to become public knowledge or possibly he was afraid that explaining the reason for the party would have given you some offense because you were not invited. In any event, this was your neighbor's business and not yours. He may not have been very friendly in refusing to share the information with you, but he was not being rude.

Auntie Mabel

The next morning I sat at the kitchen table and stared at my cereal as if it had the reported capacity of tea leaves to tell the future. I hadn't slept well the night before, and when I did sleep, I dreamt I was the captain of a sailing ship desperately looking for the lighthouse that marked the entrance to a harbor. I kept scanning the coast but found no sign of light. I thought I knew where the harbor was, but I couldn't decide whether to risk slipping past the rocks in the darkness.

Sometimes dreams require elaborate interpretations, but this one was laughable in its obviousness. My relationships, if you could call them that, since breaking up with Farantello had been brief, somewhat pleasant afternoon sails, where my hand was firmly on the tiller and I knew exactly where the boat was going and when the trip would end. Now I was involved in something that was beyond my control or Nick's. We were heading into uncharted waters propelled by winds that we couldn't direct. It was exciting. There was a sense of anticipation that included a mixture of fear and arousal. But I also sensed a certain slipperiness underfoot. Like walking on ice, I felt that each moment held the potential for me to skim along gracefully or fall flat on my face. The chances of success didn't seem to be worth the risk.

"Be sure to bring something warm. It can be cold in the hills in April," Ronnie said, bursting into the kitchen, all dressed for work and launching directly into conversation. She paused and stared at me. "Gee, you look like hell."

"Thanks. That could be because I didn't get much sleep."

"But you were in bed when I got home."

"Couldn't sleep."

"How was your date with Nick?"

"Pretend date," I corrected her automatically.

"So how was it?"

"He loves me." I couldn't believe I had just blurted it out like that, but I had to tell someone, and who better than Ronnie.

Ronnie's mouth formed a large circle. "Do you love him?" she asked after she recovered.

"I'm not even sure I like him. In fact, I'm not sure that I like anyone much right now, including you for setting up this afternoon in the woods."

"You always were a little cranky first thing in the morning," Ronnie said, dropping a couple of pieces of bread in the toaster.

"And now you tell me that it will be cold as heck up there. What should I bring, my parka?"

"Bring whatever you'll look good in. After all, now you've got a man to impress."

I muttered something rude.

Ronnie sat down and buttered her barely tan toast. "I knew that you and Nick would hit it off eventually. Didn't I tell you that? I knew the two of you would get together."

"We aren't together yet. And once we've got Sebastian convinced that I'm not the least bit interested in him, so he can settle down in connubial bliss with Bibi, we will probably not be together."

"Don't be so sure," Ronnie said, eating the center out of the toast and leaving the crust, a habit that usually didn't bother me but that morning it made me want to scream.

"I'm sure. Now go to work. I'll meet you at Everett's around one. By the way, did you get in touch with Bibi and Sebastian?"

"I talked to Bibi last night. She said they would be there."

After Ronnie left, I toyed with the idea of taking the entire day off from work. I thought I'd earned a day off, but I knew I couldn't get back to sleep, and a morning at home would only give me further opportunity to think about my situation. I would just spend more time wondering whether Nick's very understanding attitude about my fears was just a ploy, an attempt by a handsome man to appear reliable. This was one time when work might provide a welcome distraction from my personal problems.

When I walked in the front door of the newspaper, Mrs. Pear was at her desk. She began making odd twitching movements with her head, to the point that I wondered if she had developed some kind of spastic condition. Finally, I followed the direction in which her head was jerking and saw that Lieutenant Laurence was seated next to my desk.

"He's been waiting for you for almost half an hour," Mrs. Pear whispered, as if I had stood him up.

"I'm right on time. Anyhow, he didn't have an appointment," I said in a return whisper loud enough to be heard in the back of a medium-sized auditorium.

"I'm sorry I didn't call first," the lieutenant said when I reached my desk. "I only decided to drop by first thing this morning. I'd like to take your tire iron for testing."

"My what?"

"The instrument in the trunk of your car that's used for removing the lug nuts from a tire if it goes flat. It's under the floor panel with the spare tire."

I settled behind my desk. "And why do you want it?"

He didn't say anything for a long moment.

"I might be willing to give it to you if you'll tell me why you want it."

"We know that both Tilson and Donovan were struck on the head by an instrument of that shape."

"So you want to conduct a test on mine to see if it's the one used to murder the two men?"

"As I told you before, you are not an active suspect. But we want to eliminate you as a possibility. It would be in your own best interest to let me have it."

I smiled at the positive spin he put on things. I was sure he'd be much happier if my tire iron turned out to be covered with the hair and brains of the two dead men.

"You aren't the only person we're checking on."

"I'm sure Nick Manning is also on your list."

Lieutenant Laurence nodded.

"Any others?" I asked.

"There might be," he said coyly.

But there probably aren't, I thought.

I tossed him the keys to my car. "Help yourself," I said with what I hoped was the nonchalance of the obviously innocent.

He nodded his thanks and headed out to the parking lot.

A few minutes later he returned my keys and said he had found my tire iron and that it would be returned to me eventually.

"I hope I don't get a flat in the meantime," I said.

"If you do," he replied, "call the police station."

A slight smile flickered across his lips as if somewhere buried deep down there lurked a sense of humor.

As soon as he left, I started working on Auntie Mabel letters so I would be caught up enough to take the afternoon off. When the phone rang, I glanced at the clock, surprised to see that it was almost eleven.

"Hi, this is Bibi," a happy voice chirped.

"Bibi Grouse?"

"How many Bibis do you know?"

"Well, I just couldn't believe it was you. You sound so happy."

"And I owe it all to you. I couldn't believe the performance you and Nick put on last night, especially Nick. Sebastian couldn't stop talking about how in love with you Nick is."

"Wonderful. I'm glad things are working out for the two of you."

"That's why I'm calling. Sebastian invited me to go down to New York for a couple of days with him. Can you imagine that? I'm free from beating more rugs and with the guy I love? But the really exciting news is that your boss came through, and Sebastian has an appointment to show some of his pieces to a man at this gallery in New York. That's the real reason we're going; if they like what he's doing, they'll take on his stuff."

"That's really great," I said, once more impressed with what Wally could do in his quiet, indirect way.

"The reason I called is that we're leaving in ten minutes, and I don't know how to get in touch with Ronnie to tell her we won't be coming this afternoon."

"No problem. I'll give her a call on her cell and let her know."

"Great. And you know, Sebastian's right. You and Nick do make a great couple. I know you were only pretending to help me, but maybe you should think about getting serious."

"I'll give it some thought. Have a good time in New York," I said, barely managing to sound polite.

The last thing I needed was more commentary on what a great couple Nick and I made.

CHAPTER 23

Dear Auntie Mabel,

My husband and I have recently retired, and I have discovered how difficult it is for us to spend so much time together. He was a business executive, and he now insists on planning out our day, wanting to know exactly what I'll be doing and when. As a more spontaneous type of person, I find this controlling behavior hard to put up with. Since he has no hobbies and few friends, he has little to do all day and expects me to include him in all my activities. As I have a large circle of friends, this is just not reasonable. He's driving me crazy.

Going Crazy

Dear Going Crazy,

It is not unusual for adjustments to be required when a couple retires, especially for the man. Much of his life has been devoted to work, and he may be at loose ends. Why don't you and your husband sit down and see if you find some activities that will take him out of the house. I'm sure there are many volunteer organizations that would be happy to have a man of his talents. If your husband refuses to try this approach, a marriage counselor might be able to help you get a handle on this situation.

Auntie Mabel

I left the office and went back home to change my clothes for the trip to Everett's. It was an early spring day outside. Up to the sixties in the sun, but quite a bit colder in the shade. I put on a turtleneck sweater with my best jeans, but carried along a wool coat in case it was a lot colder up in the hills. I still had Ronnie's directions, which this time I knew enough to turn upside down, so I got to Everett's in about forty-five minutes. Three cars were already parked by the circle in front of the steps to the house. I recognized one of them as Ronnie's Lexus, so I pulled in next to that. As I walked up the stairs I thought about how much had happened in the few days since I was here last. Two murders had occurred, and my relationship with Nick had changed from the adversarial to something else, although I wasn't exactly sure what.

I rang the bell next to Everett's front door, and a moment later Nick greeted me. He was wearing a knit shirt and jeans with a pair of worn running shoes. He looked every inch the jock. I found it hard to keep in mind that he was also an architect, a man with an educated, artistic side.

"Everett's out on the patio with Ronnie, trying to figure out how to get the grill working. Williams, the butler, has the day off."

We went inside and headed down the hall to the patio.

"Is there usually a staff out here?" I asked.

"There's a maintenance man who lives a few miles away. He plows the road and checks out the house in the winter. Otherwise, Williams and a cook come out from Boston when Everett is here. They employ a cleaning service to do everything else. Everett told Williams and the cook to stay in Boston because we could take care of this ourselves."

I nodded, wondering if we could. It might be hard to find things in a house this size. "How much time does Everett spend here?"

"Not much. He might come out a couple of times in the spring and summer. But now that he's met Ronnie, the place might see some more use. Of course, that will only be until the new house is built."

"Has Everett found a piece of property yet?"

Nick shook his head.

"You don't seem very concerned, for the architect who's going to be building the house."

"To tell you the truth, I wish Everett would change his mind about the whole thing. He doesn't really need a place out here at all. He's got a great townhouse in Boston where he spends most of his time. I think he's just got romantic associations with the area right now."

Out on the patio, Everett and Ronnie were standing side-by-side, apparently trying to figure out how to work the giant gas grill.

"I think you turn this knob, then that one," Ronnie said, studying the directions.

Everett gave it a try and a flame appeared.

"That's a good sign," Nick said. "I wonder where Bibi and Sebastian are."

"They're going down to New York. I tried to call you on your cell, but got switched to voice mail," I said to Ronnie.

"Yeah, I was busy." Ronnie gave Everett a little smile, and I decided not to ask what kind of business that might have been. Probably it involved canoodling, to use Williams's term.

I told them about Sebastian's chance of getting into a gallery with Wally's help.

"Well, I never cared much for the little guy," Nick said. "But I guess he is a real artist."

"Oh, he's not so bad when you get used to him," I said.

"Well, why don't we get the steaks and put them on," Ronnie suggested. "I have some potatoes baking in the oven, and we'll make a salad."

We all headed inside and made our way to the big old kitchen that occupied much of the rear of the house. Nick and Everett retrieved the steaks and took them outside, while Ronnie and I began cutting up vegetables for a salad. Everything went surprisingly smoothly, and in half an hour we were sitting around a table on the patio eating our dinner. A chill breeze came along once in a while, making me wonder if I should put on my coat, but when the air was still, the warmth of the sun actually made it quite comfortable. It was one of those days when you feel that you're standing right on the border between two seasons.

"I never got to do this as a boy," Everett suddenly said.

"What's that?" I asked.

"Eat outside."

"Didn't you come out here in the summer with your grandmother?" asked Ronnie.

"Oh, sure. I spent most of the summer out here, but she wouldn't let me eat outside. We always had breakfast and dinner together in the dining room. Lunch I could have by myself in the kitchen. But she didn't think it was proper for people to eat outside, unless they were on a formal picnic."

"Still, it must have been fun to have all these woods and fields to run around in," I said.

Everett's face was sad. "Not when you're a child, and there are no other kids around. What fun is it to have all this when there's no one to play with?"

"That's all over now," Ronnie said brightly, grabbing his hand. Everett's smile immediately returned.

I was relieved to see that my comment hadn't spoiled the lunch. Everett was really "the poor little rich boy" who'd had everything except a loving family life. He'd obviously been badly injured by his cold grandmother and her bizarre approach to childrearing.

We finished the meal talking about their marriage plans. Ronnie and Everett proposed that they be married at the new house once it was complete, while Nick tried to discourage them from using that timetable by pointing out how many problems could arise to delay construction. I could tell that quite soon Nick was going to have to seriously raise his reservations about building a new house.

I volunteered Nick and myself to do the cleanup. Ronnie grabbed Everett's hand and suggested a walk in the woods. As the two of them headed down a path leading from the patio into the woods, Nick and I carried in what remained of the lunch.

"So what do you think?" I asked as we started washing up in the kitchen.

"About what?"

"Ronnie and Everett."

Nick shrugged. "They seem to be made for each other."

"So you're warming toward Ronnie?"

"Apparently she makes Everett happy, and from what he tells me, she's refused all the expensive gifts he's tried to shower on her. That makes her unique among his girlfriends."

"Poor Everett. He went from one group of people paid by his grandmother to pretend to love him when he was a child to another group that took money to pretend the same thing when he was an adult."

"Everett's actually pretty sensitive when it comes to spotting that sort of thing. Sometimes he'll play along with a mercenary woman just to have company, but he can usually tell when someone likes his money more than him. And he seems to believe that Ronnie genuinely cares for him."

"So now you have no objections to their getting married?"

Nick looked out the window at the trees just starting to show their early light green leaves.

"I don't know that I have objections. It's just that I'm not sure Ronnie realizes the level of dedication needed to keep

Everett on an even keel day in and day out. He has his really dark times. Right now it's all fun and games, but I wonder if it will be too much for her a year or so down the line."

I stayed silent. I'd never say anything negative about Ronnie, but the same question had occurred to me. We worked in companionable silence for a few moments.

"I want to thank you again for making me see the light about Max. I never should have taken that job," Nick said.

"You were right when you said he'd have gotten a different architect if you had turned him down, or he would have attempted to design the place on his own. When a man like Donovan gets his mind set on something, nothing is going to stop him."

"I suppose. And he happened to catch me at the right time when I thought I needed a job to prove to the firm that I can pull my own weight." Nick reached over and gave my arm a squeeze. "Thanks for keeping me from getting known as the architect who designed the hideous house that Max planned."

"Don't blame yourself too much. You never fully realized what Max had in mind."

"After knowing him for five minutes, I should have guessed. I turned a blind eye because I really wanted the commission. It doesn't look like there's enough business around here for me to stay with the firm in Springfield."

"Where will you go?"

Nick sighed. "I guess I'll see if one of the larger operations in Boston might have a place for me. But that would be a step back to where I started out in Chicago. I'd be another guy on a team putting up large commercial structures, and I came out here because I was trying to get away from that. What I really want to design are houses and small commercial buildings. Things that I can be in control of and put my personal stamp on."

"And you'd have to move," I said, surprised at the wave of disappointment I felt.

"I guess I would. I can't see myself commuting to Boston from here. And when a big project gets going, you can't always confine yourselves to eight-hour days. When you get through working at seven or eight at night, the last thing you want to face is a two-hour drive home."

I didn't say anything.

"Would it matter to you if I moved away?" Nick asked.

"It would spoil our little plan to fool Sebastian."

"Sounds to me like Bibi's already got that under control, if Krank is taking her to New York. As long as she can pretend to show some interest in art, she's got it made."

I knew Nick was waiting for a serious answer. This wasn't the time to be glib, clever, cool, or intellectual. He needed and deserved a straight, unambiguous reply. How would I feel if Nick went out of my life completely? A week ago I hadn't known him and I'd thought I was happy. Couldn't I easily go back to feeling that way again? I felt an emptiness inside at the idea of not having Nick around. Apparently tired of waiting for an answer, Nick started to turn away.

"I would miss you," I said.

He turned back to me with a smile.

"Really?"

"Cross my heart and hope to die."

In an instant Nick's arms were around me and his lips were pressing hard on mine.

"Help!"

Nick took a step back.

"You didn't just call for help, did you?"

"My mouth was otherwise engaged."

"Help!"

The call was faint but at the same time urgent, like someone afraid to speak too loudly but still desperate to attract attention.

"That sounded like it was from somewhere in back of the house," Nick said.

We went out the side door off the kitchen and around to the rear of the house. As we turned the corner, we saw Ronnie and Everett standing about twenty feet from the house with their backs toward the building. In front of them was the largest black bear I had ever seen.

"You go inside, I'll stay here and distract it," Everett said to Ronnie.

"No, you go inside first. I'll stay here," Ronnie said.

How long this argument had been going on, we didn't know, but the bear was obviously getting tired, because it lifted its nose in the air and ambled a couple of steps closer to them.

"Don't argue with me," Everett said in a nervous tone. "You go inside."

"Not without you."

An elbow poked me in the side and I jumped.

"That's what the bear wants," Nick said.

I looked in the direction of his finger and saw the garbage cans lined up along the house.

"Everett and I threw the meat wrappers and some scraps of meat in there right before lunch. I'll bet we didn't put the lid on tight enough."

"What can we do?"

"They could probably both move toward the door and the bear probably wouldn't bother them. He just wants to get at that can. But I think the two of them are pretty much frozen in place."

Nick moved away from me and edged along the back of the house, not taking his eyes off the bear. When he got to the row of garbage cans, he examined them all carefully. Finally, he found one with a loose lid. He looked inside then turned back to me.

"This is the one," he said. He lifted it out of the line and began carrying it at an angle past Ronnie and Everett and toward the bear.

The bear raised his head and regarded Nick with renewed interest. Gently placing the can on the ground, Nick gave it a good shove with his foot. Fortunately there was a slight downhill slope away from the house, and the can slowly rolled closer to the bear. Curious now, the bear moved toward it.

"Everybody into the house. Now!" Nick said, not turning away from the bear.

Ronnie and Everett stared, not moving. I ran forward and grabbed them each by an arm and began pulling them toward the side of the house. That seemed to wake them up, and they began to move. The bear had stuck its head in the can and emerged with a cellophane wrapper, examining it for signs of food.

When Ronnie and Everett were behind me and heading for the side door, I said, "Okay, Nick, everyone's safe."

Keeping his eyes fixed on the bear, who was clearly starting to lose interest in the can, Nick began backing up. When he finally turned the corner of the house, we both ran for the side door just as the bear decided to come closer to the house to examine the other cans.

When we got inside, we heard raised voices in the kitchen.

"Why didn't you go in when I said to?" Everett was saying angrily.

"Because I wasn't going to leave you alone out there with that bear," Ronnie replied.

"Well, I'm the man."

"Big deal. That doesn't mean that bear wouldn't eat you."

"I was just trying to look after you," Everett said more gently.

"I know," Ronnie said more softly.

Then the absence of sound suggested that they were making up their little disagreement without words.

"So, what do you think?" I asked.

"About what?" Nick said, smiling wearily as he leaned against the wall.

"Did that prove something about Ronnie and Everett?"

"You mean beyond the fact that they have about as much common sense as two babes in the woods? If they had just moved away from those garbage cans, the bear would have left them alone."

"But they didn't know that. They must have been frightened out of their minds, and yet neither one of them would leave the other."

Nick sighed. "They're idiots, but they love each other."

"Of course they do, they both did something really heroic out there today. And they did it for each other. That's got to prove they're really a devoted couple."

"Okay," Nick said with a smile. "But what about me? After all, I saved everybody. Doesn't that make me a hero as well?"

"But you weren't nearly as frightened as they were."

"My heart rate got up there," Nick said.

He really was a bit pale, and his hand shook slightly. I felt insensitive for not noticing sooner.

"Then I guess you deserve a reward, too," I said, moving toward him.

Chapter 24

Dear Auntie Mabel,

I own a large German shepherd. I am not its first owner. I got the dog through a friend in another state who got him from someone else. My guess is that somewhere along the way, Pluto was trained as a guard dog. He is the sweetest creature imaginable with the family, but if a stranger comes on the property, Pluto becomes very excited and threatening. I usually keep him chained when he's outside, but the other day my next door neighbor was coming up the walk and Pluto got loose. He bit my neighbor on his leg and would have done worse if I hadn't been there to call him off. Fortunately, my neighbor wasn't badly injured, and he agreed not to call the police. We all love the dog, but this can't happen again. What should I do?

Despairing Dog Lover

Dear Despairing,

You're right to think that a repeat of this incident would be a disaster. You would be open to civil and possible criminal action, and the dog would most certainly be destroyed. In the short term, I would be careful to make certain that Pluto is properly tied up when outside. In the long run, I would recommend taking Pluto to a professional dog trainer. Somewhere along the way Pluto learned this behavior, and it is possible that it can be mitigated if not completely unlearned. If this does not prove possible, then you must be careful to keep Pluto confined whenever *he is outdoors if you wish him to continue as a member of your family.*

Auntie Mabel

The next morning I sat at my desk, sipping coffee out of my "Have a Wonderful Day" mug, and wondered how the heck my life had gotten so out of control. In less than a week I had become a sometime suspect in two murders and become involved with a handsome man. At least one of these problems had to go away, and the one I was certain I wanted to disappear was being a murder suspect. Solving the Tilson and Donovan murders would do that, and it would give me a very good story. I had the beginnings of a hypothesis, but needed someone to run it past for flaws. I would probably have talked it over with Russ, but he wasn't in. I'd seen Wally slip down the hall to his office half an hour earlier carrying a long parcel with him, no doubt some other item for one of his hobbies. I decided that maybe I'd bounce some ideas off him.

I walked down the hall, glancing in at Sam Aaronson, who, as usual, was squinting at his computer screen. I knocked gently on Wally's door. Not hearing a response, I opened the door and stepped inside. Two barrels were pointed directly at me, huge tunnels sucking me inside. I felt my stomach muscles tighten. I opened my mouth, but for a second nothing came out. Finally, I managed to take in a deep breath and speak.

"What the hell's going on, Wally?" I practically shouted.

He seemed to awaken as if from a dream. He immediately pointed the weapon away from me.

"Oh, I'm so sorry," he said, getting up from his desk and rushing toward me. "Are you all right?"

I took another deep breath. "I guess so. I was only a bit shocked for a moment. Didn't you hear me knock? Why were you pointing that gun at the door?"

Wally put an arm around me and herded me toward the chair

in front of his desk.

"I'm afraid I didn't hear you. I was meditating."

"Meditating with a rifle in front of your face?"

"It's not a rifle, it's a shotgun. Part of my interest in duck hunting."

"I see. But why the meditating?"

"I've been reading this book. He waved a paperback in front of me: *Zen and the Art of the Shotgun*."

"What does it tell you, that you should become one with the shotgun?"

"You've read it?" Wally asked in surprise.

I shook my head. "Just a guess."

"Well, basically, you're right. You are supposed to hold the gun in the same position as you would to shoot it, but control your breathing, as you would while meditating. At the same time, you gradually come to know the trigger, until the gun seems to go off by itself, hitting the target."

"It isn't loaded, is it?"

"I don't think so," Wally said with less conviction than I would have liked.

I sighed. "I came to see you because Lieutenant Laurence has taken my tire iron."

Wally looked puzzled for a moment. "Is that a koan of some sort? Koans are puzzles that . . ."

"I know what they are, and that's not what it is," I said, cutting him off. I then went on to fill him in on exactly why my tire iron was currently at the state police lab.

"Under the circumstance one can see why he took your tire iron," Wally said.

"But he should know that neither Nick nor I had a really good reason to kill Max."

Wally shrugged as if he wasn't so sure.

"Well, we certainly didn't have a strong reason to kill Merv Tilson."

"He hit you with a rock and fought with Mr. Manning."

"But that's not enough of a reason to kill someone."

Wally gave another of his infuriating shrugs. "What you need is a suspect with a better motive."

"Exactly," I exclaimed. "And I think the key to all this is Tilson."

"How do you mean?"

"I think Tilson saw something one night while he was sitting at the bar in the Collins Inn."

"Saw what?"

"I don't know for sure. But he had a clear view of the lobby and the registration desk."

"So you think he saw somebody there who didn't belong?"

"Or a couple. Tilson's girlfriend came to see me yesterday, and she said that he had been bringing home five thousand dollars extra for the past few weeks."

"You think he was blackmailing someone?"

I nodded.

Wally leaned back in his chair, put his hands behind his head, and sucked his lips in and out for a moment like a fish.

"He didn't know any people in town well enough to blackmail them, so it must have been somebody he knew from Boston."

"Right. I figured that maybe he saw Max with another woman."

"But then Max got murdered," Wally pointed out.

"Right. So now I'm starting to think that he saw Victoria Donovan with another man."

Wally began to gently stroke the stock of the gun. "She'd be taking quite a risk. If Donovan found out, he'd drop her fast. And if he could prove adultery, she'd probably stand to lose a lot of money in the divorce settlement."

"That would give her a motive to kill Tilson. She's smart enough to know that a blackmailer isn't likely to stay quiet forever. Eventually she won't be able to pay, and he'll go to her husband."

"But do you see her beating in Tilson's head with a tire iron?"

I paused. "No, but her boyfriend might."

"Okay, let's say the boyfriend does in Tilson. Why kill Donovan?"

"Because he finds out about her infidelity."

"How? With Tilson dead, how does he find out about his wife's adventures at the Collins Inn?"

"I don't know," I admitted. "And I don't know who the boyfriend is, either."

Wally went back to his fish-breathing. Suddenly, his eyes popped open.

"Perhaps you could set a trap. Why don't you get in touch with Mrs. Donovan and pretend to be Tilson's girlfriend? You could claim to have the same information that your boyfriend had and offer to keep quiet for a price. You can expect them to pay even more, because now they've got two murder charges hanging over their heads."

"Won't they just try to kill me instead of paying me? That seems to be the way they do things."

"That's just the point. We'll catch them right before they kill you."

I stared at Wally for a long moment, not sure I'd heard him correctly. "That sounds a little risky. Shouldn't we run this by the police and let them set it up? I'm sure they have a policewoman trained for this sort of thing."

Wally shrugged. "Do you think Lieutenant Laurence is going to listen to what you have to say?"

"Farantello might."

"But he isn't in charge, and I don't think he's going to go off the reservation on this one. It could get him in a lot of trouble."

"I don't think any of this is going to stand up in court. Victoria and her guy could just say they wanted to find out who was trying to blackmail her. We could end up being the ones getting arrested."

"Once we know who Victoria's lover is, this whole thing will fall into place. And the police will probably be able to find plenty of evidence showing that this guy did it. He might still have the tire iron he used on Tilson and Donovan. They'll probably recognize him at the Collins Inn."

"So what do we do when the killer turns up and decides to go for three?"

Wally lifted the shotgun off his desk. "I tell him to make my day."

An hour later I was sitting at my desk, still not having answered one more Auntie Mabel letter.

You should pay attention to the job at hand, Auntie Mable warned me. *A wandering mind accomplishes nothing.*

"Do you mind?" I said to her. "I'm trying to decide whether to stake my life on Wally's crazy scheme."

The police are equipped to do this sort of thing. You aren't.

She had a point there, but on the other hand the police hadn't been exactly cordial to me lately. Also, this would give me a wonderful opportunity to be on the scene and write a riveting firsthand account of capturing a murderer. With Wally and his shotgun in my corner, what could possibly go wrong? On the other hand, most plans that ended in disaster had probably been developed in this same atmosphere of optimism.

With a trembling hand and a heartbeat so rapid it almost took away my ability to speak, I picked up the prepaid cell phone Wally had just purchased for purposes of anonymity. I told Wally this seemed to be going a bit far, but he just winked.

Covering the receiver with Wally's handkerchief to disguise my voice, I made my call to Victoria's cell.

The phone rang until I thought I was going to be shunted to voice mail. Then Victoria answered.

"Hello," I said weakly. "You don't know me, but I was a very good friend of Merv Tilson."

"Yes?" The voice was cool, noncommittal. Willing to hear more, but not about to rush into things.

"Merv had been bringing home some extra money lately. Money he told me he got from you." She didn't say anything, so I went on quickly, made nervous by her silence. "He told me some things about you that you wouldn't want anyone to know."

"What kind of things?"

"About you and a man who isn't your husband meeting at the Collins Inn."

There was a brief, sharp intake of breath on the end of the line.

"What do you want?"

"The same thing Merv was getting, only double."

"Why should I give you double?"

"Because now it's murder."

There was a long moment of silence on the line. "Where do you want to meet?"

"In the parking lot of the *Ravensford Chronicle*. Nine o'clock tonight."

Wally and I had decided that we wanted to be on familiar territory.

"You're in Ravensford?" Her voice rose in surprise.

Damn, we hadn't thought about that. Why would Merv, who lived in the Boston area, have a girlfriend in Ravensford?

"Yeah, we met while he was working out here," I improvised.

"So he's only known you what? Two or three weeks."

I could hear the suspicion in her voice. She was thinking

Merv wouldn't tell some woman he'd known for a couple of weeks about his golden goose. She was right; he hadn't even told the woman he was living with. Merv wasn't the kind to share information.

"Three weeks," I said, trying to sound defensive. "But he really cared about me."

This time the silence on the other end of the line was doubtful.

"If Merv didn't tell me this stuff, how would I know?" I said in a challenging tone.

Another small sigh. "Okay, tonight in the parking lot of the *Chronicle*. That's a long drive for me. Make sure you show up."

"I'll be there," I said and quickly hung up the phone.

I walked down the hall and knocked on Wally's door. A voice invited me in and he put aside the book he was reading. I stood in front of his desk like a student reporting to her teacher.

"I made the call. She'll meet us in the parking lot at nine o'clock."

"Very good," Wally said, smiling.

"Are you sure we shouldn't let the police in on this?"

"They'd only stop us."

Maybe we should be stopped, I wanted to say, but the enthusiasm on Wally's face told me he'd be very disappointed in me if I called the police. His eyes were sparkling. He was picturing himself as one of his ancient Assyrians slashing his way through the enemy army.

"I hope you don't have to use that thing," I said, looking at the shotgun.

"The threat of force will be enough," he said with way more confidence than I felt.

I was back at my desk and had just taken another letter from the Super Save More bag. I had begun to formulate my response when the phone rang. I jumped, wondering if Victoria had somehow managed to trace the call back to me. Then I realized that it was my desk phone that was ringing.

"Hello," I said weakly.

"Hello, yourself. It's Nick."

"Hi, Nick." I tried to sound enthusiastic.

"I was wondering if you were free tonight for dinner."

"Sorry, but I've got to work."

"Covering a meeting of some city board?"

"No, just a lot of stuff I have to catch up on in the office."

"Are you sure you won't have time later on? We could go out for a drink."

"Sorry, but I think this is going to drag on. It's something I have to do for Wally."

"No problem. I'll give you a call tomorrow."

After I hung up I thought how much happier I would be if I were looking forward to a date with Nick instead of a date with a killer.

CHAPTER 25

Dear Auntie Mabel,

My sister is a slob. Even though my mother raised us both to be neat and clean, her teachings apparently only stuck with me. Now in her mid-twenties, my sister's house is always messy. Things are strewn around as if the place had just been robbed, and her kitchen is so thick with grease and dirt that you're afraid to touch anything. So far I have avoided saying much about this to her because I don't want to create a rift between us, but I know that someday soon it is all going to pour out of me. Part of the problem is that she has two children and works, as do I, but she has to learn to manage her time more effectively. Is there anything I can say to her before I explode?

Living on the Edge

Dear Living,

Exploding will not be helpful to your sister, and it may well lead to bad feelings. She is obviously a woman who is at her wits end trying to cope with all of her responsibilities. It might be more helpful if you made a positive suggestion to help alleviate her situations, such as recommending a cleaning agency. Arrange to meet her at places other than her home. Ultimately, however, your sister's life is hers to live either in cleanliness or squalor. Get over it if you want to remain close.

Auntie Mabel

It gets cold at night in April. Wally and I had waited in his office until eight forty-five, then I left by the rear door. I took my time walking around the building, still not sure this was a good plan. I stopped for a few minutes to give the matter some thought. Wally and I hadn't done much talking while waiting. Wally had continued to read about how to be one with the shotgun, while I tried to become one with myself. I knew this was a dangerous plan and I was letting Wally talk me into something that went against my own good sense. I still thought so as I walked slowly around the building. Even with all my delaying tactics, I got there ten minutes early.

I stood in the parking lot under a light, so Victoria Donovan would be able to see me. I had the collar of my coat pulled up so she wouldn't be able to recognize me until she got close. A car went past on the street and turned into a public parking lot a half block away. A few minutes later I heard the click of high heels and saw Victoria leave the sidewalk and walk toward me. When she was about fifteen feet away, she stopped as if confused.

"Laura Magee? Are you the one . . ."

"Yeah," I said, "I'm the one you're here to see."

She laughed. "Don't tell me you were involved with Merv Tilson."

"I wasn't."

"Then how did you find out everything?"

"I asked around."

Victoria was silent for a minute. "It couldn't have been that easy."

"It wasn't that hard," I said. "Now do you have an envelope for me?"

Victoria took an envelope out of the inside of her coat and walked toward me.

"I don't believe you would do this for the money."

She looked out into the darkness as if searching for something.

"But you might do it to play girl detective." She reached in her pocket and a small, shiny chrome gun appeared in her hand. She pointed it directly at me. "Come on out, whoever you are. The game is over."

Nothing happened. I began to wonder if Wally had fallen asleep on watch, or if he had also read a book on Zen and the art of bluffing.

Finally, he came out from behind a parked car and walked toward us with the shotgun pointed at Victoria.

"Shoot Laura, and I blow you into small pieces," he said in what I could swear was a western drawl.

"Looks like we have a standoff," Victoria said calmly. "I shoot her then you shoot me. I don't think you want it to go that way."

"You shoot her with that tiny gun, and odds are she'll live. I shoot you with this, and you're spread all over the parking lot."

"Wally?" I said. I didn't like the way this discussion was going. Even getting shot with a small gun sounded painful and dangerous.

A car door slammed across the street. We all glanced in that direction and watched Russ Jones cross the street and walk toward us. I breathed a sigh of relief. We had another team member in the game, hopefully someone a bit more balanced than Wally.

"What's going on?" he asked with a puzzled expression on his face.

"Victoria Donovan was involved in the murder of Tilson and her husband," I explained. "Call the police."

Russ walked over to Wally. "I don't have my cell phone with me. Do you have yours?"

Wally nodded, not taking is eyes off of Victoria. "It's in my jacket pocket. Take it out."

Russ reached over with his right hand toward Wally's pocket then with his left hand he grabbed the barrel of the shotgun, jerking it upward and pulling the gun away from Wally.

"What the hell are you doing?" Wally asked when Russ turned the shotgun and pointed it at him.

"I think we've just found out who Victoria's lover is," I said. "And the murderer of Tilson and Donovan."

"Be quiet," Russ said, pointing the shotgun at me.

"What are we going to do with them?" Victoria asked, still keeping her gun pointed at me.

"We'll have to get rid of them. They know too much."

"Two more murders? This is getting out of hand."

"Do you have a better idea?"

There was a long silence, during which I hoped Victoria could come up with a better idea. But as the silence stretched out, my hopes sank.

"I didn't think so," Russ said with a note of triumph in his voice.

Suddenly a car pulled into the parking lot and Nick jumped out.

"What's going on here?" he demanded.

"Stay right where you are," Russ ordered, pointing the shotgun at him.

Nick froze in place.

"Move over next to Laura," Russ ordered, jerking the shotgun barrel in my direction.

"Now there's three of them," Victoria Donovan said with a little whine in her voice.

"We'll use the newspaper van. We'll put them all in back and go to a more rural spot. I've got the keys. You'll have to keep the gun on them while I bring the van around. Can you do that?"

"Okay."

Russ lowered the shotgun and began to walk to the back of the parking lot to get the van. As he started to move, a figure detached itself from the darkness near the building, moving toward him. When the figure walked under the streetlight, I could see that it was Farantello, and that he had his gun pointed directly at Russ.

"Put down the shotgun," he said.

Russ smiled. "You're not going to shoot me, because Victoria has a gun on your ex-girlfriend. Shoot me, and she'll shoot Laura."

"I don't think she will," Farantello said in a reasonable tone. "In fact, I bet right now she's figuring out how she can make this look like all these murders were all your doing."

"What are you talking about?" Russ asked.

"Well, I doubt that Victoria bashed Tilson and Donovan over the head. That was you. And I'll bet she's wondering how she can claim she never knew you were going to do anything as violent as that."

"We planned it together."

"Oh, I have no doubt of that. But once Victoria gets a high-priced lawyer, I'll bet the story changes. But if Victoria shoots Laura, well, there's no way she can claim that was your fault. So I'm betting she's not going to shoot Laura. So you'd better put the shotgun down right now."

Russ looked over his shoulder at Victoria.

"Victoria?"

The only answer was the sound of her gun dropping onto the pavement.

Another figure came out of the darkness near Victoria. He walked over, picked up the gun, and began to cuff the woman.

"Who's that?" Wally asked.

"That's my sergeant. He came here to shoot Victoria if she didn't drop the gun."

"Sounds like you had all the angles covered," Wally said in

admiration.

Farantello just looked at the man and shook his head.

Two hours later we were all sitting in the newsroom, minus Victoria and Russell, who had been taken down to police headquarters by Lieutenant Laurence. Speaking of Lieutenant Laurence, he had been furious, to put it mildly, at the plan Wally and I had hatched to catch the killers. He kept threatening to charge us with interfering in a police investigation, but since our interference had solved the case, as Farantello pointed out, it looked like we were going to be let off the hook with a stern warning.

As Farantello had predicted, once separated from Russell, Mrs. Donovan painted a picture of a lover who was so crazed by the need to have her that he killed two men without her knowledge. I wasn't sure how her story would play in court, but those of us in the newsroom got a good chuckle out of it.

The truth, as far as we understood the slippery concept, was that Russell and Victoria had indeed been lovers for a long time, going back to his years in Boston. Victoria had met him through one of her charities when they got the attractive anchorman to host one of their fundraisers. Max Donovan had also known Russell, but had never caught on to his relationship with his wife. The problems began for the happy couple when Russell made his ill-timed remarks before an open mike and got fired. When the only job he could lasso in the communications business was here in Ravensford, the logistical problem of how they could still see each other arose for Russ and Victoria. Victoria knew she could make the jaunt to Ravensford only so many times before some slip-up would happen, and Max would spot it. That was when Victoria began working on Max with the idea of having a second home in the town where he grew up. Playing on his weakness for self-promotion, she convinced him that he'd be showing his old friends exactly how far he had come by building a striking house.

Since Max spent a good deal of time on the road, Victoria figured she could frequently stay at the second house during his jaunts and meet with her paramour. All of this might have worked out if Max hadn't assigned Merv Tilson to the work site. As I had discovered, Merv spotted Victoria Donovan checking into the Collins Inn at a time when her husband was away on travel. One thing Merv had in abundance was patience, particularly when he had a beer in his hand, and although they didn't check in together, Merv eventually spotted Russell Jones going up the stairs at the inn a half hour after Victoria and leaving shortly before she did. An inveterate watcher of Boston television news, Merv recognized Russ, and gradually took to following him around in the evening, spotting him once again going to the Collins Inn right after Victoria checked in and leaving shortly before she checked out.

Doubtless, Merv couldn't believe his luck, and so began the blackmail, which inevitably led to the first murder. Although she didn't come right out and admit it, ending her marriage without a sizeable divorce settlement didn't sit well with Victoria. Since Russell hoped to share one day in that bounty, he was willing to do the dirty deed. Unfortunately, at the same time this was going on, Max was running into difficulties with his house plans due to his remarkably bad taste. But the final blow to their plans came when Max spent his last night alive in the Collins Inn where, as we learned later, Millicent Collins happily informed him that his wife often stayed. This came as a surprise to Max, who immediately called his wife and demanded an explanation as to why she was visiting Ravensford while he was out of town. Given Max's doggedness, Victoria and Russ knew that eventually the truth would come out unless they acted.

According to Victoria, Russ, his appetite already whetted by one murder, decided it was time to get rid of Max once and for all. This would allow them to be together and also provide Victoria with a nice chunk of Max's holdings. Using his trusty tire iron, Russ carried out the scheme. The flaw in their plan was that neither of them knew about Merv's girlfriend. If they had known, I'm sure she would have been a third casualty. Russ probably dumped Tilson's body at the work site because he was aware of Max's conflict with the neighbors, and thought it would muddy the waters and suggest Frank Taylor's involvement. Max's body ended up in the newspaper parking lot because he had overheard the argument Nick and I had with Max. And, by the way, Russ's lack of interest in getting involved in that fight with Max wasn't due to cowardice, but was based on the fact that Max would have recognized him, and any connection between himself and Max was the last thing Russ wanted made public. Finally, Nick had happened on the scene only because he wanted to see me. Apparently he'd just received a job offer from an architectural firm in Boston, and he rushed over to tell me about it, ending up right in the middle of a real live Mexican standoff. Some days you just don't know what you're getting into.

Oh, yeah, I almost forgot. The reason Farantello showed up is because, as I was walking around the newspaper building to meet with Victoria, I decided that Wally was out of his mind, and there was no way we were going to pull off this stunt by ourselves. So I gave Farantello a call. Lieutenant Laurence was at home. Farantello called him. Then, with his sergeant in tow, he came along to save my life. Farantello doesn't let on much, but I can tell that he was pretty happy to be the one to wrap this up.

I'm pretty happy it turned out the way it did, too. I got a terrific story, and I'm still alive.

CHAPTER 26

Dear Auntie Mabel,

My boyfriend and I are getting married in May. We've been living together for two years, and his mother says because of that it wouldn't be appropriate for me to wear a white wedding dress. I think she's just being old-fashioned. What do you think?

Wants White

Dear Wants White,

Although there is a traditional connection between virginity and a white dress, there have been lots of non-virgins, both public and private ones, who have worn white down through the years. In my opinion you should wear whatever color looks best on you and the heck with what people think.

Auntie Mabel

Nick and I stood in front of Everett's summer cottage and watched the cars pour in. This time an army of professional valets were in charge of parking, so Nick and I just stood there talking.

"How's the job in Boston going?" I asked.

"Pretty much as I expected. I'm part of a big team putting up commercial buildings. But I've got some feelers out in case a smaller firm in Boston is looking for someone."

I nodded. Nick and I had stayed in touch by phone for the first couple of months after he moved to Boston, but then, as we both had expected, the calls became fewer and finally stopped. This was the first time we'd talked in three months. Our relationship simply hadn't had enough time to take root before his move. When people asked, anyway, that was the story I gave them. It fit the facts, but the facts, as usual, concealed more than they revealed. Although we never actually talked about it, I knew Nick's failure to protect me the night of the murderers' arrest made him feel inadequate. I never thought that way. What could he have done? Silly male pride, you might say, but silly or not, it contaminated our relationship, killing it before it had a chance to bloom. Nick being who he was, every time he looked at me, he saw his own shame.

We were together now only because Ronnie and Everett were getting married today, and Nick was the best man, while I was the maid of honor. Nick had managed to talk Everett out of building a new house. I think the clincher had been when Ronnie said they could make the old house a new one by having children and giving them a happy life there.

I could see Everett standing up by the front door in a close conversation with Sebastian, who was waving his hands artistically. Sebastian was doing well with his sales from that New York gallery, but once a salesman always a salesman.

"Is Sebastian really trying to talk Everett into putting a bear sculpture in the back on the spot where that big one frightened them?"

Nick smiled. "I wouldn't worry. Even if Everett weakens, Ronnie won't let him give in. She'll buy something from Sebastian to put in a museum somewhere with her and Everett's names on it as donors, but nothing of Sebastian's is going on this property if she has anything to say about it. The natural beauty is enough."

"Good for her. She's become a real fan of nature."

"That's why she bought that piece of land from Max

Donovan's estate and signed it over to the city as a park."

"Yeah. That brought the whole story to a nice close."

A few minutes later we were all arranged, ready to proceed through the house and onto the patio where the wedding was to be held. As I stepped out into the bright sunshine, I was blinded for a moment. When I was able to see again, there was Farantello sitting in the audience, grinning at me. I smiled back. He and his wife had finally decided that as much as they loved their daughter, pleasing her wasn't a good reason for them to try to force the pieces of their marriage back together again. He'd recently asked me if I would consider going out with him again, even though he'd acted like a fool. I told him I'd think about it.

I think he knew what my answer was going to be. I certainly did.

ABOUT THE AUTHOR

Glen Ebisch has had over a dozen mysteries published for both young people and adults. He lives with his wife in western Massachusetts. His interests include philosophy, yoga, and reading mysteries.